One Hot ROOMIE

Hot Brits, Book Two

ANNA DURAND

JACOBSVILLE BOOKS JB MARIETTA, OHIO`

ONE HOT ROOMIE

ISBN: 978-1-949406-30-6 (paperback)
ISBN: 978-1-949406-31-3 (audiobook)

Manufactured in the United States.

Jacobsville Books
www.JacobsvilleBooks.com

Publisher's Cataloging-in-Publication Data
provided by Five Rainbows Cataloging Services

Names: Durand, Anna.
Title: One hot roomie / Anna Durand.
Description: Marietta, OH : Jacobsville Books, 2020. | Series: Hot Brits, bk. 2.
Identifiers: ISBN 978-1-949406-30-6 (paperback) | ISBN 978-1-949406-31-3 (audiobook)
Subjects: LCSH: Roommates--Fiction. | Virgins--Fiction. | British--Fiction. | New York (N.Y.)--Fiction. | Romance fiction. | BISAC: FICTION / Romance / Contemporary. | FICTION / Romance / Romantic Comedy. | FICTION / Romance / New Adult. | GSAFD: Love stories.
Classification: LCC PS3604.U724 O55 2020 (print) | LCC PS3604.U724 (ebook) | DDC 813/.6--dc23.

Praise for Anna Durand's Books

" I loved the slow-burn, should we-shouldn't we, what's right, dilemma and desire that built and built until the steam had to escape. [*One Hot Chance*] is equal parts fun, steam, and moral quandary. [...] I am in love with Chance and his brothers already."

MaryLou Hoffman, Page Princess blog

"[*Lethal in a Kilt* is] full of hot sex, adventure, and so much laughter. I found myself laughing-out-loud at the antics of the Witches of Ballachulish (Logan's sisters) and the hilarious flirting and sexy banter between Serena and Logan. [...] Recommend highly! "

Sharon Clayton, The Eclectic Review

"*[Insatiable in a Kilt*] smokes from the very first pages... Durand's characters are a delight and seeing how they mix business with their increasing attraction for each other is entertaining indeed. [...] Durand's Hot Scots family saga just keeps on getting better."

Readers' Favorite

"I loved the Scottish in Ian and the strength of Rae, but the love of one little girl makes [*Notorious in a Kilt*] something to behold."

Coffee Time Romance

"*Gift-Wrapped in a Kilt* is a marvelous continuation of the author's MacTaggart family saga. Durand's story has an entertaining plot, and her steamy interludes are well-written...a celebration of healthy relationships between loving adults written in a tasteful and compelling manner."

Readers' Favorite

"I have enjoyed this whole series, but Emery and Rory [from *Scandalous in a Kilt]* have stolen my heart and are now my favorites!"

The Romance Reviews

"An enthralling story. [...] I highly recommend the writing of Ms. Durand and *Wicked in a Kilt*, but be warned you will find yourself addicted and want your own Hot Scot."

Coffee Time Romance & More

"There's a huge hero's and heroine's journey [in *Dangerous in a Kilt*] that I quite enjoyed, not to mention the hot sex, and again, not to mention the sweet seduction of the Scotsman who pulls out all the stops to get Erica to love him."

Manic Readers

Other Books by Anna Durand

One Hot Chance (Hot Brits, Book One)
Natural Passion (Au Naturel Trilogy, Book One)
Natural Impulse (Au Naturel Trilogy, Book Two)
Dangerous in a Kilt (Hot Scots, Book One)
Wicked in a Kilt (Hot Scots, Book Two)
Scandalous in a Kilt (Hot Scots, Book Three)
The MacTaggart Brothers Trilogy (Hot Scots, Books 1-3)
Gift-Wrapped in a Kilt (Hot Scots, Book Four)
Notorious in a Kilt (Hot Scots, Book Five)
Insatiable in a Kilt (Hot Scots, Book Six)
Lethal in a Kilt (Hot Scots, Book Seven)
Irresistible in a Kilt (Hot Scots, Book Eight)
Fired Up (standalone romance)
The Mortal Falls (Undercover Elementals, Book One)
The Mortal Fires (Undercover Elementals, Book Two)
The Mortal Tempest (Undercover Elementals, Book Three)
The Janusite Trilogy (Undercover Elementals, Books 1-3)
Obsidian Hunger (Undercover Elementals, Book Four)
Willpower (Psychic Crossroads, Book One)
Intuition (Psychic Crossroads, Book Two)
Kinetic (Psychic Crossroads, Book Three)
Passion Never Dies: The Complete Reborn Series
Reborn to Die (Reborn, Part One)
Reborn to Burn (Reborn, Part Two)
Reborn to Avenge (Reborn, Part Three)
Reborn to Conquer (Reborn, Part Four)

Chapter One

Reese

I dig the key out of my pocket and unlock the door, pushing it open to walk into my new flat—temporary flat, loaned to me by my brother's fiancée, for the sole purpose of finding an American girl to shag. All right, maybe that isn't the reason I gave Chance and Elena. My brother and his almost wife wouldn't have lent me this flat otherwise. When I'd announced to Dane, my other brother, that I was going to shag an American girl, no one took me seriously. Everyone heard me shout it, but they know I love to make jokes.

This time, I'm not joking. That's my plan. Find, win over, and sleep with a New York woman.

Why not? It's a bit of fun, nothing more. A holiday from my life which has started to, as my almost sister-in-law might say, suck royally.

"Another hot British guy in the Big Apple," Elena had said when she and Chance saw me off at the airport, for my big holiday in the US. "Try not to leave a trail of broken hearts. You Dixon boys are impossible to resist."

My brother found a wife in America, but I'm not after that. Women never want to date me, much less marry me, because they know I'm good for one thing. All I need is a girl in my bed.

Well, the bed is optional.

I drop my bag on the floor beside the sofa and turn in a circle to get the full view of my new temporary home. Elena's flat, which she told me Americans call an apartment, has big windows with a view of the city. She says at night the view is spectacular, with all the skyscrapers glowing with lights. I suppose that view might help me win over an American girl. It can't hurt.

A bar separates the living room from the kitchen, where I see the refrigerator, the cooker—ah, the oven—and all the other items a kitchen is meant to have. Elena told me her brother Kyle, a college student, had left the refrigerator stocked with beer in case he wanted to stay here for a weekend now and then as a break from living on campus. Elena also said she left food in the fridge for me, so I won't have to live on beer. She gave me the numbers for all the best takeaway restaurants in the area too.

Elena called them takeout restaurants. I need to remember these American words if I'm going to impress the ladies instead of confusing them. Chance warned me about that problem.

He and Elena are getting married in fourteen days, in New Hampshire of all places. It's where they live now. That means I have two weeks to make my American dream come true. I jumped on a plane the day after Elena offered me her flat. Chance paid for my ticket because it was expensive to get a last-minute flight and because I'm, well, financially challenged at the moment.

Losing my job has that effect. Not my fault I'm unemployed. Sometimes it just happens, and yeah, it royally sucks.

I drop onto the sofa, stretching out lengthwise on the very puffy cushions. Elena and Kyle used to share this flat, and they've left all the furniture. That includes the sofa, two equally puffy chairs, and a table. I cross my ankles, link my hands behind my head, and sigh with contentment. Closing my eyes, I begin to formulate a plan for hunting down eligible women.

"Oh!"

A feminine voice bursts out with that exclamation.

I spring off the sofa, as surprised by the intruder as she seems to be by me. The girl has on nothing but a sleeveless white top and plaid knickers that barely cover her arse. Her honey-brown eyes are so wide with shock that I wonder if they'll pop out of their sockets.

She shakes her head furiously, making the ponytail she's gathered her blonde hair into flap like a dog's tail. "No, no, don't rape me. I'm a virgin."

"What? I—You're the intruder."

"Am not. I have a key."

"So do I." Raising the key, I wave it in the air. "Here it is."

This girl is pretty, and she's got a body I'd love to touch and kiss and lick all over. Maybe I've already found my American girl to shag.

If' she'll stop accusing me of being a sexual predator.

"Kyle said I could have the place," she says. "So go. Scoot."

"Elena and Chance invited me to stay here. Alone." I inch closer but stop when her eyes get even wider. "Ring Elena and ask. She'll tell you."

The girl eyes me, her mouth contorting into the most endearing look of suspicion and curiosity. She hurries to the bar, leaning over it to grab something off the kitchen counter. The movement makes her tiny knickers slip down just enough to give me a glimpse of her arse cheeks.

She straightens, now holding a mobile phone, and taps its screen several times. Holding the phone to her ear, she keeps her suspicious gaze trained on me. "Your aura looks okay, but I better check with—Hey Elena, it's me. Did you invite some British guy to stay here? At your apartment. What? Kyle said I could."

I watch her lips pucker while she listens to whatever Elena is telling her.

"Ugh, that Kyle." The girl rolls her eyes. "He's a sweetie but such a dufus sometimes." She eyes me again. "Are you sure he's safe? Yeah, of course, but… Uh-huh. You're the one who told me I'm too trusting. How do I know this really is Reese Dixon?"

Though I'm missing half the conversation, I can guess most of what's going on. Elena is explaining to her friend that I'm not a psychotic sex offender who escaped from prison an hour ago and is desperate to get a leg over with the first female he sees.

I might be gagging for it, but not because I'm a predator. I've been experiencing a bit of a drought lately.

"Okay," the girl says. She holds her phone away from her face to peer at the screen. Her gaze flicks to me and then back to the screen. She sighs and tells Elena, "I guess he is who he claims to be. Thanks, hon."

She hangs up, sets her phone on the bar, and walks up to me. She tips her head back to meet my gaze.

The sexy little American offers me her hand. "I'm Arden Clover Pesti. It's nice to meet you, Reese Dixon."

I shake her hand, loving how soft and warm her skin is. She smells good too, like powder and cocoa butter. "It's nice to meet you too. Arden, is it? That's an unusual name, especially for a girl."

"Yeah, it's weird, I know. Blame my parents. They're big-time hippies, even though the hippie thing ended in, like, nineteen seventy-seven."

"Hippies?"

"Flower children, bohemians, beatniks, et cetera."

"I know what the word means." I love that she's keeping her hand in mine, even though the greetings are over. Her skin is like porcelain, with the faintest freckles on it. "Are you friends with Elena, then? Or just Kyle?"

"Elena is my BFF. We're like this." She pulls her palm away from mine so she can link the fingers of both hands in a locking gesture. "We're tight. Inseparable. I mean, except for the past nine months when I was in Ecuador with the Peace Corps."

"That's an admirable thing to do."

She shrugs. "I wanted to see the world, so I joined up. All I ever saw was Ecuador."

I scratch the back of my neck, wincing slightly. "Sorry I scared you. Elena said I'd have the place to myself."

"The Linwoods have definitely got some crossed wires going on."

Although Kyle Linwood had left beer in the apartment, it was Elena who'd told me that. I never actually spoke to Kyle. The Linwoods got their wires crossed for sure.

Arden smiles sweetly at me, swinging her hands at her sides. "Elena mentioned you've never been to America before."

"That's right. My brother has lived here for a long time, but I never got round to visiting him."

"Well then." She spreads her arms wide and grins. "Welcome to the United States of America and to New York City."

I can't help chuckling. She's so unbelievably adorable.

"Thank you," I say. "I feel at home already."

She comes closer, standing on her toes to look me in the eye, and her expression turns serious. "New York is awesome, but there are a few things to watch out for. Cabbies will be obnoxious. It's their way. Never buy a falafel from a street vendor who has facial hair. Never have a mixed drink, unless you want to get roofied." She leans in more, her nose almost brushing mine. "And watch out for the greys. They'll sneak up on you while you're sleeping, so keep a can of mace by your bed."

When she uses the term greys, I get the impression she's not talking about hair, which leaves me hopelessly confused.

"Oh," she says, popping upright and holding up a finger, "I almost forgot. Never flush the toilet on a Tuesday before eight a.m."

"I see." I don't, not even a little, but I'm enjoying listening to her lovely voice. She can tell me any barmy thing she wants, and I'll listen without saying a word. "I appreciate the advice."

She nods, seeming satisfied. Then she wanders off down the hall that Elena told me leads to a bathroom and two bedrooms.

Greys? What the bloody hell is that sexy, barmy girl on about?

I ring Elena to ask. "Arden told me to watch out for greys, but I have no idea what that means. I didn't want to offend her by asking."

Elena laughs. "She's a hoot, isn't she? You'll get used to her. Arden's the smartest person I've ever known, next to Chance, but she can be a little kooky."

"Are you going to tell me what greys are?"

"Maybe I should let you figure that out on your own. Or you could ask Arden. She's not easily offended."

In the background of the call, I hear my brother's voice, but I can't understand what he's saying.

"Gotta go," Elena says, "Chance needs me. He's completely hopeless when it comes to picking out place settings for the wedding, but we have to do that before we fly to England tomorrow."

"Isn't midnight an odd time to shop for place settings?" I have no idea what those are, but it sounds like a daytime shopping event.

"Yeah, but we tried shopping in the store this afternoon. Chance kept getting distracted by shiny objects like big-screen TVs. Online shopping is the only way to keep him focused."

Elena and I say goodbye, and I carry my bag down the hall.

Arden dashes out of one of the bedrooms, holding a length of aluminium foil in her hand.

"Here," she says, offering the foil to me. "You might want to sleep with that over your head to keep the microwaves from altering your brain chemistry. The waves are strongest at night."

What else can I do? Her earnest expression convinces me she's serious, so I take the foil. "Thank you. It's kind of you to look out for my brain chemistry."

I watch her perfect arse wiggle while she spins around and trots back into her room. She shuts the door, cutting off my view of her bum.

Oh yes, I'd love to shag that girl. So what if she's barking mad? I'm not going to date her, much less marry her.

Maybe my American adventure begins right now.

Chapter Two

Arden

I'm not totally insane, I swear it. Yes, I love weird things like auras and aliens, and sometimes I go a little overboard in telling people about them. It's become a kind of self-defense mechanism. I mean, after a dozen guys try to seduce you so they can try to get their grubby hands on your money, you tend to get a little paranoid. Babbling about my kooky interests turns out to be the quickest way to get rid of those losers. I don't believe everything I say, though I do believe in the possibilities of things that can never be proved. Sometimes I accidentally scare off a solid prospect with my weirdness. C'est la vie.

Yeah, those three words are the extent of my French expertise. And I got those from a Robbie Nevil song. Oh, that reminds me. I'm also obsessed with eighties pop music. So, I'm super popular on karaoke night but pretty much treated like a plague victim the rest of the time.

I flop backward onto my bed, making it bounce and creak.

Bright side? I have the most amazing best friend in the world. Elena Linwood, soon to be Elena Dixon, has always appreciated my loony side. I adore her to pieces. And her fiancé? Whew, break out the firehose. I haven't met Chance Dixon yet, but I've seen pictures of him. Not only is he smokin' hot, but according to Elena, he's also great at his job and a super nice and super fun person. She's so lucky, and I'm so happy for her.

As for Chance's brothers, I wasn't supposed to meet them until the wedding two weeks from now. Elena told me they're hot too, but that Dane is the cerebral type and Reese wants to "shag" an American girl. If I were going to walk into the living room in my undies and bump into one of them, I would've hoped for Dane. Instead, I got Reese. The hound. The one who finds women's numbers on restroom stalls and calls them. Seriously. Elena told me that.

But Reese has the most beautiful blue eyes, and I'd love to push my fingers into that thick, dark hair. Can't forget about his body either. Holy shit, he's hot. And while I was in Ecuador, I had lots of time to think about stuff and decide I don't want to be a virgin anymore. I want to have sex as soon as possible, preferably with a decent guy.

I sigh miserably, flinging my arms out like a snow angel without the snow. Reese is gorgeous, but in addition to what Elena told me about him, I'm getting a vibe from him that screams "player." How did Elena get so damn lucky with Chance?

Well, they did start out having a quickie in an elevator...

My tummy grumbles. I'd been on my way to the kitchen for a snack when Reese scared the holy living shit out of me. Maybe he's gone into his room by now. Maybe I can sneak out there and grab something to eat.

When did I become a coward? Me, the girl who bungee-jumped off a bridge. And participated in a midnight seance. And chased UFOs across the Mojave Desert. Of course, those lights in the sky had turned out to be drones operated by bored teenagers. C'est la vie, as my motto goes. Nothing ventured, no adventure gained.

I pull on my favorite T-shirt—the one that features a glow-in-the-dark alien face—and my favorite pair of shorts. They're pink, naturally, but they don't glow in the dark. I have panties that do that, though.

Appropriately dressed, I amble out into the living room.

Reese is sitting on the sofa, staring down at his phone. He smiles and types something, then notices me.

"There you are, Luscious," he says, like that adjective is my name. "Did you finally remember why you came into the living room the first time?"

"Yes. I'm hungry."

I sashay past him—honestly, sashaying is my normal way of walking, can't help it—and don't look at him. In the kitchen, I open the fridge to consider its contents. Beer. Lots of beer. *Jeez, Kyle, are you a lush or what?* Elena left some food, so I look past the four six-packs of Coors and a twelve-pack of Budweiser to decide what I want to eat. It's all healthy food, like hummus and yogurt. My tummy demands decadence, not diet stuff.

Reese comes up alongside me, peering into the fridge. "Don't you have any biscuits?"

"Do you see any cookies? I'm not hiding them in my undies."

He smiles at me, the expression full of sly humor. "You know what biscuits are. Damn that Chance. How can I confuse you the way he did with Elena if you already know all the British words? It's not fair at all."

"Trust me, I'm plenty confused."

"But I meant to charm you with my Britishisms." He glances at my skimpy shorts, his gaze traveling up to my slightly oversize T-shirt and its alien face—and to my breasts. "I want to charm the fuck out of you, Luscious."

Oh yeah, my player vibe is screaming again.

"My name is Arden." I hook a finger under his chin, lifting it until he has no choice but to look at my face. "Arden Clover Pesti. Not Luscious. Got it?"

"If you insist."

"Thank you."

He jams his hands in his jeans pockets and peers into the fridge again. "How can a girl who sleeps with aluminium foil on her head be so uptight?"

"Alu-what? I guess that's British for aluminum foil." I fold my arms over my chest. "I'm not uptight. But I don't know you, and nicknames are things friends or relatives give each other."

"Fair point." He shuts the fridge. "I'll hold off on calling you Luscious."

"I appreciate that. Now, do you like pizza?"

"Yes, I love it. Love a good takeaway, full stop."

"Takeaway's British for takeout, right?"

"Yes."

"Okeydokey," I say, turning toward the bar, where the landline phone is. "I'll order some pizza."

Reese excuses himself to go unpack and change into different clothes. The stuff he's wearing looks fine to me, but whatever. I make the pizza call and sit down on the sofa to wait for the delivery to arrive. Reese comes out of his room a few minutes later and takes a seat at the other end of the sofa from me. He's wearing pajama pants and a T-shirt that has a red rose on it with the words "England Rugby" underneath it.

Pointing at his shirt, I say, "Guess you're a rugby fan."

"Yes, but I also played rugby at school."

"Let me guess. You were the star player."

He shrugs, almost seeming shy about it. "Maybe I was, but it's a team sport. Couldn't have won games by myself."

"Is rugby like soccer?"

"Similar, but with differences. And we call that other sport football, not soccer." He glances down at his clothes. "I almost wore my Manchester United shirt."

I probably look confused. Manchester what? Honestly, why do British people assume Americans understand them?

Reese smiles. "Manchester United is a football team."

"And by football, you mean soccer."

He rolls his eyes, huffing. "No, I mean football. You Americans have a bloody stupid idea of what that word means."

"And you Brits are so damn arrogant about your sports. I mean, it's only a game."

"*Only* a game?" He gapes at me like I've suggested the sun is nothing more than a forty-watt light bulb. "Don't tell Kyle you said that. He worships American football and is obsessed with stock car racing."

"Yeah, I know. That's why I've never dated Kyle, besides the fact he's my best friend's brother."

I prop my feet on the coffee table, crossing my ankles.

Reese rakes his gaze all the way down my body to my feet and back up again. "Please tell me you were joking about being a virgin. You said that to stop me from attacking you, right?"

"Not completely. I am a virgin."

I've had orgasms, lots and lots of them, but only my hands have ever touched me down there. Sometimes I really want to pop that cherry, but men are such dicks. Most of them. The good ones are, of course, already taken.

"Does Elena know that?" Reese asks.

"That I'm a virgin? Yeah. My family knows too, since we talk about pretty much everything."

His lips curve into a wicked smirk. "Do you want to stay a virgin? Because I'm the best first time you'll ever have."

"Not exactly humble, though, are you?" I lean back and shake my head. "Sorry, I've taken a vow to stay untouched until I meet the man I'm going to marry."

That's baloney, since I've decided to get laid ASAP, but I'm trying to discourage Reese.

Uh, why am I doing that? He's hot, I'm horny, and we're both adults.

But he's also the brother of my best friend's fiancé. My brain keeps telling me that makes it wrong somehow, but my body thinks that's bullshit.

He sighs with immense sarcasm at my claim I'm waiting for marriage. "What a shame."

"The right guy is worth waiting for."

"Hmm." He braces his elbow on the sofa's back, raising his hand to rest his chin on it. "Who is your perfect man?"

"Don't know. Someone who"—doesn't care about my money or my pedigree—"treats me with respect and love. A man who adores me. You know, the kind who always considers my feelings and does whatever he can to make me feel appreciated and loved."

"You want a gay man, then?"

"No." I give him a fake scowl. "I want a good man."

"I'm very good. Ask any of the girls I've been with."

"Sex isn't part of the formula for a good man. I mean, I want to have sex with the guy I marry, but that's not the most important thing."

Reese studies me like he's trying to figure out what kind of alien species I belong to, his eyes faintly squinted and his lips faintly puckered. "You really are barking mad."

"Excuse me? I'm quirky, not crazy."

"Oh, don't get me wrong." He scoots a little closer, his voice lowering to the sexiest rumble I've ever heard. "I'd love to get a leg over with you. And I guarantee you'll be glad you gave up your innocence to become a sinner with me. I do sin better than anyone."

He is cute. A real hunk of man candy. And he smells soooo good. Is that cologne or aftershave? The spicy scent of it wafted over me when he leaned in, and now I can't stop smelling it. My nether regions love that aroma, and how close his lips are to mine. I'm getting slick and warm and deliciously achy.

"Thank you for the offer," I force myself to say. "But I'm good the way I am."

"Yes, I agree. You are perfect, lush—" He stops short of calling me Luscious again and frowns a little. "Is it all right if I call you darling? Or is that too close to the word I'm not allowed to use?"

Oh what the hell. It's not like I'll jump his bones if he calls me that word again.

"Go on," I say, waving my hand like I'm a queen granting my royal permission. "Call me Luscious."

He grins. "Thank you."

"Whatever."

The doorbell rings, and Reese springs off the sofa to get our food. He returns a minute later with a large pizza box and sets it on the coffee table, then flips the lid up.

His brows draw together over his nose. "They must've bollocksed up the order."

I shimmy closer to the sofa's edge, rubbing my hands together and humming with hungry delight as I lay eyes on our snack. "Mm, yummy. They got it exactly right."

"But this isn't pizza." Reese lifts a slice, eying it like teeth might erupt out of it to bite his nose off. "No cheese. No meat. It's some sort of pastry crust with what looks like applesauce all over it."

"Yep. It's an apple strudel pizza." I grab a slice and take a bite, moaning because it tastes sooooooo good. Cinnamon and sugar and apples, all mushed into one warm, gooey slice of food heaven. I close my eyes while I chew, moaning some more because, damn, I'm so hungry and this is like an orgasm in my mouth. After I swallow my large bite, I say, "Try some. It's the most delicious thing I've ever put in my mouth."

Reese says nothing. He sits there with a slice of gooey goodness in his hand, but he's not staring at the pizza. He's staring at me.

"What's wrong?" I ask. "Don't you like strudel?"

"I love it," he says, his voice huskier and deeper, the sound of it shivering heat through me. "But I'd rather devour you."

"No sex. Remember? I'm staying a virgin until—"

"Then you shouldn't consume dessert pizza like you're about to climax." He sets down his slice and inches closer to me. "A bloke only has so much willpower, you know."

I gaze into his hooded eyes for a long, long moment, struck by the intensity of his desire for me. No guy has ever looked at me that way. Suddenly, I want to toss the pizza and mount him right here on the sofa. Reese Dixon might prove to be the biggest temptation I've ever laid eyes on, and I'm having trouble remembering why I need to discourage him.

Twenty-eight years old and still untouched. Maybe a night of hot, meaningless sex with Reese Dixon is what I need to help me unwind after nine months of living with an Ecuadorian family.

Sleeping with Reese wouldn't be simple sex, though, would it? His family and my friend make it complicated as hell.

In my mind, I mutter a thousand nasty curses as I leap off the sofa and retrieve a plate and a can of beer from the kitchen. While Reese watches me with a curious expression, I slap three pieces of strudel pizza onto the plate and march back to my room. Okay, maybe I'm sashaying. Like I said, that's my normal way of moving, and I can't help it.

Though I might be exaggerating it a little to torture Reese.

Chapter Three

Reese

Arden is gone when I wake up in the morning. Her bedroom door is open, and her bed is neatly made, but she's not there. I wander into the kitchen and find a note taped to the refrigerator. It says, "Out getting breakfast. You're welcome." I can't decide if she's saying "you're welcome" because she's bringing breakfast home for me too or if she wrote that strictly because she's off her rocker.

I sort of like her insanity. It's adorable, in a very strange and slightly disturbing way.

While I wait for Arden to bring food—I assume that was the meaning of her note, not that she's out eating at a cafe while I'm starving to death here—I have a shower and then ring my brother Chance. Since his almost wife and almost brother-in-law got me into this mess, I decide he should be the one to fix it. *Find me another flat*, I plan to tell him.

But as I'm scrolling down my list of contacts to find Chance's number, I reflect on last night and the sexy little American dressed in nothing but her underwear. Maybe I don't want to move. Yet. Not until I see if I can get Arden naked and make that hot body sweat and writhe. She's a virgin and my almost sister-in-law's best friend. Does that make it wrong to seduce her?

Probably. But what if…

I growl at myself, because even I'm not that much of an arse, and tap my phone's screen to dial Chance's number.

"What's wrong?" Chance asks, his tone giving away the fact he's smirking from the safety of our parents' house in the English countryside, too far away for me to tackle him to the ground for being cheeky.

"Nothing's wrong," I say. "Didn't Elena tell you about the Linwood family blunder?"

"Yes, and I assumed you would be a gentleman and get yourself to a hotel."

"Why would you assume that? It's me you're talking to. Reese, not Dane the boring and uptight brother. It's me, the fun one in the family."

"Right. What was I thinking?" Chance sighs. "Please don't harass Arden. I haven't met her yet, but Elena loves the girl to bits. If you do your usual shag-and-run routine, my fiancée will not be pleased."

"What sort of dick do you think I am? I never run. I kiss them goodbye and walk out the door at a normal pace."

"Elena told me Arden is, ah, not like the other women you've been with."

I drop onto the sofa. "Do you mean because she's barmy, or because she's a virgin?"

"Both." Chance pauses. "Arden told you she's a virgin?"

"Yes." I relate last night's surprise to Chance and finish up by saying, "So you can see why I want to stay here. She's a charming nutter and the sexiest girl I've ever seen."

"Leave her alone, Reese."

I hate it when he uses his big brother voice. I feel like a schoolboy who got caught stealing girls' bras and shrinking them in the clothes dryer.

And yes, I've done that. Not in ages, though.

But if I shrink Arden's knickers, they'll be almost nonexistent. Hmm… That's not a half bad idea.

"Don't do it," Chance chastises.

"What?"

He huffs, part humor, part big brother bossiness. "Whatever it is you're thinking of doing. Keep your randy paws off Arden."

"Fine, I will. But don't blame me if the girl tears my clothes off."

"That happens to you all the time, doesn't it? Women going into a sexual frenzy the second they see you. I should call the New York Police Department and warn them of the danger."

"Ha-ha." I grumble, because I know Chance is right and I should keep my randy paws off Arden Clover Pesti. Christ, even her name is oddly arousing. "You trusted me enough to let Elena lend me her apartment, so trust me not to deflower her best friend."

"All right. I'm sure you can't get into too much trouble in two weeks. Then, you'll be in New Hampshire for the wedding, where I can see you."

"Yes, yes, you've done your bloody annoying big brother thing." I hear someone fiddling with the lock on the apartment door and sit forward, feeling bizarrely excited at the prospect of seeing Arden again. "Got to go. See you in New Hampshire, and kiss Elena for me."

"I will."

Though Chance can't see it, I smirk as I say, "Make it a good, deep kiss. From me."

"Bugger off, Reese."

He hangs up on me.

I still hear noises from the door, like Arden is having trouble getting it unlocked, so I rush over there and open the door.

She stumbles into me, her left arm laden with two eco-friendly reusable canvas sacks, while with her right hand she grips the door key. The sharp end of the key stabs me in the gut, but it doesn't really hurt. Not much, anyway. Her entire body careens into me, her breasts mashed against my chest and the top of her head nudging my chin. The shopping sacks seem about to fall out of her grasp, so I hug her to me tighter, strictly to stop her from dropping the sacks.

Yes, that's why I hold on to her luscious little body. For the safety of her groceries.

But she feels so good, so warm and soft but with ample muscle tone. And she smells incredible too. Not like perfume or some other scented whatever, but like it's just the way this woman smells. And it makes my cock wake up.

I ease her away from me and take the sacks. "Are you all right?"

"Me?" she says, staring at me with a vaguely dazed expression. "I stabbed you. Are you okay?"

"You stabbed me with a key, and I don't think those are usually fatal." I smile, and because I'm holding her sacks in one arm, I can pat my belly when I add, "See? Right as rain."

"I've never understood that saying. What's so perfectly right about rain?"

"Don't know." I nod toward the kitchen. "Am I taking your groceries there?"

"Yes, please. Thank you for carrying them."

"I might be a louse, but I'm not rude."

She shuts the door and follows me into the kitchen, where I set the sacks on the counter. Arden starts taking items out and lining them up on the counter in neat little rows.

Leaning against the counter, I can't help watching her and smiling. "Are you obsessive-compulsive?"

"No. I like neatness, that's all. Why be messy? There's no purpose to it."

"You won't like living with me, then. I toss my clothes everywhere and never touch a feather duster."

"Uh-huh. I can see that about you." She flashes me a playful smile, but then turns serious. "Why did you call yourself a louse?"

"It was a joke. But I do love women, and I usually leave as soon as we've both come."

"You mean you screw them, pat them on the head, and walk out the door."

That's almost exactly what I said to Chance, but without the head-patting. How does this girl I've known for five minutes understand that about me? Maybe she receives microwave thought transmissions.

She raises her brows, like she's expecting a response to her assessment of me.

And I suddenly feel itchy all over. "Yes. I kiss them, then I walk out."

"Why?"

I start to scratch my arm but stop myself. Trying not to look at her, I pretend ignorance. "Why what?"

Evasion is always a good choice when a woman pokes her charming little nose into your affairs. Not that I've had any affairs. It's strictly been come-and-go for me. And I don't mean "come" as in walking into the bedroom. Once we've both gotten off, what else is there to do but leave?

Arden stops unpacking her groceries and turns to face me, crossing her arms over her chest. "Why are you afraid of relationships?"

"I am not afraid. Relationships aren't for everyone, you know."

Her lips pucker while she roves her assessing gaze over all of me. "That's what people who are afraid of falling in love say. They usually have some kind of trauma in the past that makes them terrified to try again."

"Sorry to disappoint you, but I'm not traumatized," I say, sounding annoyed because, bloody hell, she is annoying me. And I'm getting itchier. Could I be allergic to interrogation? "Can we please stop talking about my sex life?"

"Sure, whatever." She resumes unloading her sacks. "I'm making banana oatmeal pancakes with your choice of Greek yogurt or syrup on top. Oh!" She pulls out what looks like a tiny milk carton, grinning. "Whipped cream too. If you're into that sort of thing."

Of course I am. I love decadence in all its countless varieties, but her grin and her sensual body are making me picture all the ways I can use whipped cream to make her squirm and gasp and finally scream my name.

No, you arse, you can't. She's off limits, remember?

Yes, yes, yes, I know that. Honestly, I do. I know I cannot touch her.

But fantasies are completely allowed. So tonight, I'll be locked in my bedroom fucking my own hand while I imagine I'm fucking her.

I stifle a groan. Being an upstanding adult is awful.

Arden has emptied her grocery sacks and proceeds to fold them, stacking them next to the refrigerator before she starts gathering the ingredients for our breakfast. I offer to help out as her cooking slave, and she cheerfully bosses me around. I love it when she smiles at me over her shoulder and says, "Mash the bananas with the potato masher, not your fingers."

"But if I use my fingers, you can lick them clean for me." Yes, flirting is also allowed. Chance didn't order me not to do that. He said to keep my hands off Arden, that's all.

Her lips twitch upward. "You have a one-track mind, don't you?"

"No, I have two tracks available at all times, running parallel." I wink. "One of them is reserved for dirty thoughts."

"Yeah, I can tell."

We go back to cooking, and soon we've got two plates loaded with banana oatmeal pancakes. A glass of milk sits next to each plate, which we've placed on the bar. Arden and I take our seats on the stools and dig in. I pour enough syrup over my pancakes to start a flash flood of stickiness, but Arden is judicious in her use of syrup. She does, however, spoon a mountain of whipped cream onto her stack.

I watch her shove four layered pieces of pancake into her mouth. "Do you believe all those barmy things you said last night?"

She swallows her huge mouthful of food. "Some of it. The part about not flushing the toilet before eight on Tuesday is pure baloney. Most of that stuff is my way of testing guys to make sure they're not schmucks."

"Did I pass the test?"

"I'd give you a B plus."

"Should I be flattered or offended by that?"

Arden pretends to consider me, her head tilted to the side. "Too early to say."

We go back to enjoying our breakfast, and once I've finished eating, I turn to Arden. "Let me wash the dishes. I insist."

"I won't argue with that." She consumes her last bite of pancake, leaving a smear of whipped cream right next to her mouth. "I like having a hot British guy as my kitchen helper."

Though I hear her words, all I can think about is licking that cream off her skin. Sweet, decadent cream. The word makes me picture her naked with my head between her legs while I taste the best kind of cream there is.

Arden lunges forward, pressing her mouth to mine.

I freeze, trying so damn hard not to kiss her back. Chance said not to touch her, but she started this. Doesn't that absolve me of any wrongdoing? She kissed me. And her mouth is silky and warm, her lips sweet from the cream clinging to her skin. I burn to taste her, to flick my tongue out and lick the cream off, then plunge my tongue into her mouth.

But I can't.

Her tongue slips out, gently probing between my lips, all but pleading for me to ravish her—or maybe for my mouth to open so she can ravish me.

I want that. Want it so badly that holding back is like a physical pain.

She pulls away just enough to speak, our mouths a hair's breadth apart. "I thought you wanted to kiss me. Was I wrong?"

"No, you're not wrong. I do want that. But..."

Damn my brother. But it's not his fault. I should've gone to a hotel.

"But what?" Arden asks.

"I can't."

"Why not?" She brushes her lips over mine, and her voice lowers to a tantalizing whisper. "I might be a virgin, but I can still kiss. I enjoy it a lot."

Now my cock is not only awake, it's clamoring for me to take her up on that offer and ravish her mouth, then her body.

I jump off my stool and trip over my own feet, grabbing the bar for support. "I promised I wouldn't."

Arden studies me, her lips caught between her teeth. "Who did you promise that to? Not me."

"Chance. He made me swear I wouldn't touch you. You're a virgin, for heaven's sake."

I spin around, meaning to run for my bedroom, but Arden grabs my arm and stops me.

"All I want is a kiss," she says, her voice hushed and sultry. "I'm not planning to have sex with you, Reese. Isn't it my choice who I kiss or don't kiss?" She moves in front of me, looping her arms around my neck and raising onto her tiptoes, her mouth so close I can almost taste her. "And I want to kiss you."

What am I meant to do? My willpower has never been that strong.

So I groan and kiss her.

Chapter Four

Arden

Reese is an incredible kisser. And I know what I'm talking about. I mean, I've been kissed a lot. His lips stay firm for a brief moment, then they soften and slide over mine, damp and with a touch of sweetness on them from our breakfast. I lick at his lips, and he teases mine right back. I sag into him, abandoning myself to the kiss, to the moment, to this virtual stranger who makes me want to taste him in every way imaginable.

I open for him, desperate for a deep kiss, and he thrusts inside to explore my mouth like he wants to spend hours doing only this, curling his tongue around mine, plowing deeper only to withdraw almost all the way. I wrap my tongue around his, loving the way he responds with a hungry groan and an equally hungry swipe of his own tongue. We dance a sensual tango with our mouths for several minutes, so long that I lose track of the time, lost to the sensations and flavors.

Reese wraps an arm around me, tugging me closer.

He feels so incredibly good, with my body mashed to him, his muscles flexing and tightening against me. He smells incredible too and tastes so delicious I never want to stop kissing him. Last night, I'd kind of thought he was one of those jerks who loves to say suggestive things to embarrass me, but this morning I've decided he's not like that. He helped me make breakfast. How many guys would do that? He makes me laugh, like when he smeared whipped cream across his upper lip and called it his "old man mustache" and invited me to "give it a lick." He grinned when he said that, so I knew he was teasing.

But I'd wanted to do that.

Reese Dixon is gorgeous and hotter than hot, sexier than any guy I've ever dated.

He shifts a hand to my ass, massaging it while he groans into my mouth.

I'm so ready for more, aroused by his kiss and his body and his… everything, to the point that I want to rip his clothes off, drag him to the floor, and screw his brains out.

He did pass my first test by not getting annoyed with my kooky antics.

Reese lets go of me and staggers backward a couple steps. His eyes are wide. His mouth gapes open while he shakes his head at me. "I can't do this. Chance… Elena… I promised…" He shakes his head harder, almost frenetically. "This is too wrong even for me. I'm sorry."

"Elena's my best friend, but she doesn't decide who I kiss." I hesitate for only a second before I say, "Or who I sleep with."

Though he still gapes at me, his brows squish together in the cutest expression of total confusion. "You want to sleep with me?"

And his voice jacks up so high on the last word that he almost squeaks it. Which is even cuter.

I giggle, because he's so darn lovable like this, not the cocky Brit who can't believe I'm a virgin, but simply a guy who's baffled by the fact I want him.

His eyes narrow, and his mouth slants into a smirk. "You dare to laugh at me? If we slept together, you'd never snicker at me again. I'm fantastic."

Yeah, I laugh some more, a little louder now. "You're just the cutest."

"Cute?" His smirk kicks up into a sly smile, and there's humor shimmering in his blue eyes. "You do realize I'll have to prove to you how not cute I am. And we will be naked while I'm providing that proof."

"I'd love that." I move closer, stopping a few inches from him, gazing up into his eyes. "I want you, Reese."

His playful cockiness fades away, replaced by a softer, surprised expression. "We met last night. Why would you want to have sex with me?"

"Do you have any idea how long I've been resisting the urge to get naked with a guy? It wasn't super hard, until now." I inch even closer, resting my palms on his chest. "Until you showed up and scared the shit out of me."

He sets his hands on my hips. "I'm not the relationship sort. If we do this, I won't stick around to cuddle with you or meet your family or any of that bollocks."

I smile. "You have to stick around. We're living in the same apartment."

"Well..." He steps back, drawing out a distance between us so my hands fall away from his chest. "I've been thinking I ought to get a room in a hotel."

"You mean Chance told you to move to a hotel."

I love Elena, so if she thinks Chance is amazing, then he must be. Elena wouldn't be marrying him otherwise. But Chance Dixon has no right to decide with whom I share an apartment or whether I screw that someone or not. So what if Reese is Chance's brother? It's still none of his beeswax.

From the moment I saw Reese, I wanted him. He's beyond sexy. And I'd decided before I left Ecuador that I want to get rid of this pesky virginity. I've waited a super long time to pop that cherry, and I don't want to wait one day longer.

Maybe nine months in a faraway country has made me a touch boy crazy.

"Please don't leave," I say. "I got back from Ecuador two days ago, and I haven't really had anyone to talk to in months. The family I lived with down there was nice, but it's not the same as having a real friend. You're fun. Sometimes full of yourself, but yeah, fun. I'd love for you to stay."

He regards me for a minute, his lips twisting this way and that, his fingers curling and uncurling.

When I think he's about to say he's leaving, he sighs and throws his hands up. "Fine. I'll stay. But I cannot have sex with you, Arden. My brother will have my hide if I do."

"Nobody needs to know. It can be our secret."

"Chance will know. Trust me." Reese ambles to the sofa and collapses onto it, then pats the cushion beside him. "Sit. Let's... talk or whatever. You should find out who I am before you toss your virginity in my lap."

I laugh while I pad over to the sofa and sit down near him. "Toss my virginity? Not sure how that works. It's not like I have an actual cherry in there that I can whip out and hand to you."

His upper lip curls. "That's the most revolting image I've ever been forced to picture."

"Yeah, I realized how gross it was while the words were spewing out of me. Sorry. I have a tendency to say inappropriate things."

"Do you?" His lips curve into a sexily teasing smile. "I think I'm going to like you, Arden Clover Pesti."

"Most people think I'm nuts."

"Well, you are slightly barmy. But it's endearing, in a strange way."

"Thank you. I love being strange."

He cocks his head like he's analyzing me. "How old are you?"

"Didn't anyone ever tell you women don't want to be asked that question? I'm surprised a player like you doesn't know that."

"I'll have you know I've never asked a woman her age before." He angles his body toward me a little. "But I'm curious to know how long you've been holding on to your virginity, and why. So, how old are you?"

"Guess that's a fair question, considering I told you I want to have sex." Get naked and crazy with him, actually, but I don't want to scare him off. "I'm twenty-eight."

"You don't act twenty-eight."

My lips twitch, but I stop myself from smiling. He seems sincere in his belief that I don't act the way someone my age should. "How do you think twenty-eight-year-olds usually behave?"

"I don't know. Less demented."

This time *his* lips twitch, and I realize he's kidding.

Crossing my arms, I lift my chin. "Okay, Mr. I'm So Hot You'll Forgive Me for Being a Smart-Ass, how old are *you*? I mean, since I answered—"

"It's all right. I'm not shy about anything." He sets one ankle on the other knee. "I'm twenty-four."

"A younger man. Wow, that's even hotter."

"Older women definitely are hotter." He winks. "Even if they're still innocent."

"Who said I'm innocent? I've had orgasms, you know. Loads of them."

His brows shoot up. "You have?"

I give him a fake chastising look and wag my finger at him. "Don't make assumptions about me. You'll almost always be wrong."

"Lesson learned." He slants forward, resting his arm on the sofa's back. In a hushed voice I'm sure is pure sarcasm, he asks, "Are you sure they're orgasms? Since you've never had sex, how would you know?"

A laugh snorts out of me. "Yeah, like there's any doubt about it when I'm writhing on my bed and can't breathe because I'm coming so hard."

He stares at me for a few seconds, without blinking, then clears his throat and sinks back into his corner of the sofa. He grabs a throw pillow and puts it on his lap. "So you, uh, self-pleasure."

Oh holy cuteness, it's so absolutely adorable that he can't seem to make himself say the word masturbate. Which makes me want to torture him a little. He deserves it after being so shocked that I'm a virgin, and so shocked that I want to have sex with him.

"I don't do it all by myself," I say. "I have Rod."

"You—" His eyes bulge like they might explode or something. "Who the bloody hell is Rod? I thought you didn't have a boyfriend. And you said you're a virgin, so how in the world could some bloke called Rod give you orgasms?"

No, I'm not lying. I do have Rod. But I might be allowing Reese to get the slightly wrong impression about my little friend.

Rod is my favorite vibrator. Yeah, I named it. I'm kooky, remember?

The human sex machine sitting on the sofa with me has stopped gawking, but he still looks flummoxed. "Does he give you oral sex?"

"No, it's more hands-on." I sigh and gaze into space, smiling a touch, like I'm remembering all the fantastic O's Rod has given me. "Rod gets me off faster than any of my other fuck buddies."

"You're what?"

And now Reese's eyes are bulging again.

Maybe I should have mercy and stop torturing him, but I'm having too much fun.

Reese scrubs a hand over his face, twice, until the shock softens into total confusion. "I think you have a very different definition of virginity than anyone else on the planet. How many fuck buddies do you have? Do you take your kit off for them?"

"What's a kit?"

"Your clothes."

"No, I keep my nightie on. But a good, hard come always leaves me zonked out, so I go to sleep right after." I act like I'm sentimental about it when I say, "As for how many fuck buddies I have... Well, there's Rod, obviously. And Big Jim, who gets the job done slower but with more intensity. And oh, I can't forget Jack. He's like a bunny rabbit, all energy and super-quick climaxes."

Reese's confusion has morphed into a suspicious expression. He eyes me like he's almost figured out what I'm talking about. "Jack is like a rabbit. Why do I feel like you're having me on in the worst way?"

"Okay, I admit it. I'm talking about my vibrators."

He blinks quickly several times before a naughty smile spreads across his face. "You have three vibrators? Quite a randy little thing, aren't you?"

"Staying a virgin doesn't mean I have no sexual urges." I tilt my head, eying him kind of the way he'd eyed me a minute ago. "How many women have you slept with?"

"Oh no, I have more sense than that. I never tell a woman the answer because no girl really wants to hear it."

"That many, huh? You're a real hound, I guess."

"I'm a ladies' man."

"Which is code for man-whore."

He scoots closer and speaks in a deeper, softer voice. "I'm experienced, which means I can guarantee you won't want Rod or Jack anymore after you've been with me."

"Awesome. Let's do it now."

"I can't perform on command like a ruddy vibrator." He shoves a hand into his hair. "I feel like we should get to know each other a little first."

"Are you always so shy about getting it on? I mean, from the way you talk, I assumed you'd be raring to go."

"This is different for me." He scrunches up his whole face and groans. "I can't do it, anyway. I promised Chance, and I don't break my word."

"Wow, you are the sweetest, most honorable man-whore I've ever met."

"Thanks. I think." He relaxes, a big breath gusting out of him. "Tell me one thing. What in the bloody hell is a grey?"

Chapter Five

Reese

I'm trying to resist Arden, honestly I am. Resistance isn't in my nature, though, not when it comes to women. And this woman is so… irresistible. I paused there because I tried to think of a different word to describe her, but nothing else came to mind. She's curvy and sensual and bizarre and barmy. Whenever she smiles, her cheeks get these sweet little dimples in them, right at the corners of her mouth, and it makes me want to kiss her again. I also love the dimple at the top of her arse, where those delectable cheeks meet. I glimpsed that dimple last night when Arden was traipsing around in her knickers.

A scrap of plaid, that's all it had been. A scrap that barely covered her bottom.

This morning, she's wearing jeans and a short-sleeve jumper, both of which cling to her alluring shape.

Sweater, not jumper. I'm in America now, so I need to remember the differences.

"Reese, are you awake?"

She's waving her hand in my face, and I realize she's been talking while I've been fantasizing about her.

"Ah, sorry," I say. "My mind wandered. What were you saying?"

"You asked me what a grey is. I explained, you missed it, and I'm not super inclined to tell you again."

"I'll listen this time. You have my word." Assuming she doesn't smile again, making that dimple reappear. All bets are off then.

All her clothes might be off too.

Except I promised Chance I wouldn't do that. Damn him. Chance has no right to tell two adults what they can and can't do. Or maybe I'm making excuses because I lust for Arden's body.

She taps my nose with her fingertip. "You're not listening again."

I realize she's right and smack my forehead. "Sorry. Don't know what's wrong with me today."

"Maybe it's jet lag."

"Could be." It's not, but at least that sounds like a good excuse for my behavior. "Let's try that again. What is a grey?"

"An alien."

I blink a few times while I watch her, because I can't believe she means what it sounds like she means. Maybe she's referring to immigrants from another country. That would make a lot more sense. Though I'm not aware of another country that has grey people in it.

She must mean grey hairs. Right? But how would that be an alien…

"What do you mean by 'an alien'?" I ask.

"An extraterrestrial being, as in a living creature from a planet other than Earth. They have grey skin, spindly arms and legs, and big black eyes."

She's looking at me like I'm the one who's a little crazy.

"Extraterrestrials," I say, still trying to come to terms with that one. "You actually believe grey aliens are visiting your bedroom in the middle of the night."

"No," she says with a faint laugh, like that's the dumbest thing she's ever heard. "Of course not. I'm not sure they abduct people either, but I completely believe alien life exists and that it's possible they've visited Earth."

"Do you really sleep with aluminium foil on your head?"

"That would make me insane, so no, I don't do that. It was part of the test, which you passed." She wiggles her bum like she's trying to get more comfortable. "Don't you believe in anything unusual? Things you haven't seen or touched yourself?"

"I believe your tits are beautiful and soft, even though I haven't touched them."

Her lips crimp like she's trying not to smile. "I offered to have sex with you, and you turned me down."

"No, I delayed making a decision." I fidget but can't get rid of what feels like a rock under my arse. I suppose it's a figment of my imagination, which is warning me to steer clear of Arden and her edible body. "I promised my brother I wouldn't touch you. He swears Elena will be devastated if I corrupt you."

"Corrupt me?" She laughs outright this time, and it lights up her expression. "You're so cute. I told you about Rod and Jack. How can you think I'm innocent and incorruptible? I have a filthy, filthy mind, and you'd probably blush if I told you the things I've imagined doing with you—and to you."

Her gaze flicks down to my cock.

And of course, that makes blood rush into it.

What has she been imagining doing to me? Since she looked down there, I'm guessing—hoping, maybe praying—she wants to get her mouth on me.

More blood rushes south.

"Let's go outside," I suggest. "For a walk. We can keep talking while we do that, and fresh air will be good for both of us."

"Sure, that sounds fab. I know a park we can go to."

"Brilliant. Let's do that."

It's a beautiful, warm morning, so we don't need coats. I try to talk Arden into wearing one, claiming I'm worried she'll catch cold when I'm actually afraid I'll snap and fuck her on the sidewalk if I have to look at her breasts cradled in whatever bra she's wearing. The fabric of her sweater stretches tight over those mounds. She won't wear a coat, so I'm probably doomed.

"Into the lift," I say when the doors open for us.

"The what?"

"Oh. Sorry. I meant elevator. I forget the American words for things."

"Don't worry about it." She walks into the elevator, and I follow. Once the doors slide shut, she asks, "Are you sleeping with anybody right now?"

I roll my eyes at her. "No, Arden, and I won't be sleeping with you either."

"But you want to." She stuffs her hands into her jeans pockets, cocking one hip. "I still don't get why you're anti-relationships. What are you afraid of?"

I make a noise that even I think sounds vaguely like a growl. "I told you earlier, I'm not afraid. Relationships aren't for everyone, you know. I remember reading somewhere that monogamy is a construct of modern civilization, but it's not natural for human beings. We need to shag lots of people in order to propagate the species."

And aren't I so fucking proud of myself for using all those big words. Won't she be so fucking impressed.

She snorts and shakes her head at me. "That's what players say to excuse their sleazy behavior. But you don't strike me as a sleazoid, so I'm guessing you have another, deep-seated reason for being afraid of commitment."

Oh yes, she's so fucking impressed. I really am an idiot, aren't I? Maybe I shouldn't have used the word shag in my little diatribe meant to convince her my lifestyle is noble.

I hope I'm not trying to convince myself of that.

Maybe there's a reason for my behavior, and I don't know what it is. Maybe I should figure that out.

Another time.

"What is a sleazoid?" I ask. "Can't tell if I should be offended until I know what on earth you're talking about. Is that another kind of alien being? Sleazoids must have red skin and forked tails to match their giant, forked dicks."

"Do you have a forked dick?" She raises up on her toes, angling her head down and peering at my crotch. "Maybe you should show me, strictly so I can decide if you really are a sleazoid."

When she moves only her eyes to peek up at me through those thick lashes, her lips kink up at the corners. It's the sexiest thing I've ever seen, and of course, my dick loves it.

Is she trying to seduce me? Little Arden Clover Pesti, the virgin who believes in aliens? I've had women seduce me before—I've always loved when that happens—but none of those other women called me a sleazoid and asked to see my forked penis as part of the seduction. It shouldn't be working on me, but it is. I want to whip out my cock and show her the proof I'm not a sleazoid from the planet Arsehole.

Arden sighs and faces the elevator doors.

Everything she does and says makes me want to call my brother. I know exactly what I'll tell him. "Bugger off, Chance, I'm shagging Arden today. Tell Elena it's not my fault her friend is the world's first nymphomaniac virgin. Cheers. See you at the wedding."

Instead, I glare at the elevator doors until they slide open. Then I shake off my irritation and follow Arden out of the building, listening while she tells me about every building and object we pass on our trip to the park. I learn all about the street vendors too, and I buy us both ice cream cones along the way. I love watching her lick that ice cream. Her pink tongue snakes out, curls around the ice cream, and glides back into her mouth with the tip rolled over. With every sensuous lick, she closes her eyes and moans.

All I can do to stave off a flaming hard-on is to cough into my fist and focus on the most disgusting image I can think of—the rotting corpse of a dead hedgehog I'd once seen in the woods near my parents' house.

The image doesn't cure my problem, but it helps a little.

When we get to the park, Arden leads me down a wide, paved path that takes us past flowering trees and park benches. We see children flying kites and older men playing some sort of game inside a court that has a glass roof over it. Arden informs me they're playing bocce. I've heard of the game, but I have no idea what's involved.

"I don't really understand the game myself," she admits when I ask her about it. "But some people really like it. I once dated a guy who was totally into bocce, and he told me it's related to a British game called bowls. No idea what that is."

"It's a very boring game where you roll little balls around and try to get them close to another little ball." I groan, remembering the times I've sat through games to be polite. "My brother Dane loves bowls. But I didn't realize bocce was the same thing."

We pass a couple of brick buildings, then Arden sits her lovely arse down on a bench and waves for me to join her. I do, but I keep an arm's length between us. Like I said, resisting temptation is not in my nature. Chance has ordered me to go against my every impulse and act as uptight as he is. Or was. He seems to have loosened up a lot since he met Elena. She must be a bloody fantastic lay.

She's also very sweet and very clever. Arden is starting to remind me of Elena, but without the business suits or the inexplicable adoration of my uptight brother. No, Arden is not stuffy. She's like a breath of fresh air that's been imbued with the essence of sunshine.

She's a free spirit. Turns out I like that.

And I keep liking that about her until she scoots across the bench, coming dangerously close to me. "Don't sit so far away. I like smelling you."

"Smelling me? Did I forget to use deodorant this morning?"

The enchanting girl laughs.

Every time Arden does that, the sound is sweet and almost musical, and it tickles my senses in the strangest way. And every time she does that, I want to kiss her until she melts in my arms.

I can't do that, though. Chance has forced me to dig out the willpower I never knew I had, so I can resist this free-spirited angel who claims to have a filthy mind.

Willpower is awful. Why does anyone want to have it? Why do people brag about theirs? It's the worst invention in the history of the universe.

Our bench sits right under a tree covered with white flowers that give off a sweet, delicate perfume. When a breeze shivers the flowers, a few petals come loose and float down to light on Arden's hair and shoulders. She looks like an angel, smiling at me with those white petals clinging to her blonde hair.

I want to strip her naked right here, lay her across the length of the bench, and push inside her supple body. No, that won't work. I can't fit on the bench that way. But I could lift her onto my lap and let her ride me.

Tossing that fantasy into the mental rubbish bin, because I've developed a terrible case of willpower, I focus on the grassy area across from us. "It's nearly lunch. Where should we eat?"

The sexy angel leans in, her nose brushing my cheek, and inhales deeply. "Mm, you really do smell yummy."

I never use cologne, so I have no idea what she thinks she smells. Maybe the body wash I used? No, not that. What then? I don't want to know, because I'm sure the answer will cure me of this willpower disease I've contracted.

And that would be a bad thing… why?

Her nose grazes my cheek again. "I could just eat you up."

All the air in my lungs splutters out of me, and I'm fairly certain I spray saliva all over the sexy woman who's sitting much too close to me.

"Why are you fighting it?" she asks. "You want me. I want you. And you did swear you'd be the best first time I could ever have."

I swallow a groan. Why did I say that last night? What kind of moron am I? Chance hadn't issued his directive yet when I told Arden I would be the best first time she could have. Now the sneaky girl is using my own words against me.

"Forget what your brother said," Arden tells me. "He has no right to interfere in my life."

"What about Elena? She'll hate me if I—you know." Now I can't even say the words. *Take your virginity.* What's hard about saying that? Nothing. But I can't make the words leave my mouth. They seem to be stuck somewhere between my brain and my throat.

Arden settles a hand on my thigh and skates it up and down, her longest finger grazing my cock.

I'm not sure she even knows she's almost touching that part of me. My dick knows, and it loves the tickling sensation. My willpower thinks it's torture. I'm on the fence. Teetering. Tipping more and more in the direction of Arden.

Straighten up, Reese, or you're a dead man.

Arden slides her hand up my thigh, over my hip, and all the way up to my chest. Her lips flutter over my earlobe when she whispers, "For nine months, I slept in a strange house with somebody else's kids down the hall, and I didn't even have my vibrators. I had nothing to do at night except listen to the parents getting it on in their room. The noises they made, all those little grunts and gasps and moans, it made me wonder why the hell I'm still a virgin. I had to give myself a happy ending every night, manually. My right hand developed a permanent cramp."

Naturally, my mind shows me a fantasy of her doing that.

"Why are you telling me this?" I ask. And why does my voice sound rough, like I've swallowed a mouthful of sandpaper? I'm having trouble breathing, and my cock is straining to get out of my trousers.

"I'm telling you," she says, in the sexiest whisper I've ever heard, "because I had decided to lose my virginity before I ever met you. But now that I have met you, I can't think of anyone else I'd rather let pop my cherry."

Though I've always hated that term, when she says it the words ignite a searing, irresistible need in me. I grip the bench so hard my fingers hurt, but even the pain can't douse my lust for Arden.

"Please, Reese," she purrs into my ear. "I want it to be you."

I want that too. More than want it. I hunger for her like a starved man who's been offered a sumptuous, succulent meal for the first time in months. And yes, I want to devour her.

But I seem to have this annoying, wriggling thing in my brain that makes me do the last thing on earth I want to do right now. I think that wriggling thing is called a conscience.

Which explains why I jump up, force a smile I'm sure looks slightly manic, and tell Arden, "I have to go. Time for me to get a hotel room. Thank you for showing me some of the city, but it's really not appropriate for me to, uh, share an apartment with you."

And I run off.

Well, I don't literally run. I walk away very, very quickly from the sensual woman on the bench who all but begged me to fuck her. I, Reese Dixon, walk away from a girl who wants sex.

Only as I'm crossing the lobby of the first hotel I find do I realize I'll have to go back to that bloody apartment to get my things. If I have any luck at all, Arden won't be there.

I'm not feeling that lucky today.

Chapter Six

Arden

When I get back to the apartment, suffering from intense sexual frustration, I grab my phone and call Elena. She's not answering her cell, so I leave a message telling her we need to talk pronto. I can't believe my best friend would tell her fiancé to order his brother not to sleep with me. I mean, it's my body. It's my choice. And if Reese is such an awful guy, why would Elena lend him her apartment? Chance must have come up with the boneheaded idea of treating me like I'm an idiot who can't make a decision for herself.

To be fair, Chance and I haven't met. He doesn't know me, but his fiancée does. What did Elena tell him? What could she say that would make him think I need protecting from his brother?

The word virgin. That makes most guys think I'm fragile.

I fume for a while, then decide to get started on the work project I don't actually need to start for a couple weeks. I'd planned on using this time before Elena and Chance's wedding to relax. She insisted I didn't need to help her with the wedding arrangements, and she wants me to take it easy since I'm freshly home from Ecuador.

New York isn't my home, but I thought I'd have more opportunities to get laid in a megacity, instead of back home in Stockbridge. My hometown in Massachusetts doesn't have a broad selection of man candy.

Work takes my mind off things for a couple hours.

Then the phone rings, and I see it's Elena calling.

"Hey, hon," I say when I pick up. "How's England today?"

"Beautiful. How are things at your end?"

"Fab. How's your British stud today? Is he plotting more ways to interfere in my life?"

Elena is silent for a few seconds. "What are you talking about?"

"Didn't Chance tell you? He ordered his brother to keep his hands off me."

"Chance did what?" Elena pauses again, but she doesn't sound confused or surprised when she speaks again. Instead, she sounds like my best friend who wants to hear all the details. "Do you want Reese's hands on you?"

"Yes, dammit, I do. And your honey is seriously messing with my plans."

"What plans do you have for Reese?"

"I want him to take my virginity. That's the plan."

Silence. For such a long time I think I've shocked my best friend so horribly that she's passed out.

Finally, Elena laughs. "Oh, those Dixon boys really do have the magic touch with the ladies, don't they? I mean, I had sex with Chance in an elevator five minutes after we met. Can't blame you for wanting to get it on with Reese. He's as hot as Chance, maybe hotter." She lowers her voice to a whisper. "Don't tell Chance I said that."

"My lips are sealed."

"You always did have a soft spot for the bad boys."

"That's because they're so much fun." I twirl a lock of my hair around my finger while I remember Reese's naughty smile when he told me he'd be the best first time I could ever have. "I like Reese. He's more fun than any guy I've met before, and I really, really want my first time to be with him. I had a sexual epiphany in Ecuador, and I don't want to wait any longer. Look, I'm not after a relationship. I know Reese isn't that kind of guy, but I'm also pretty sure sex with him will be incredible. Don't I deserve a rockin' first time?"

"Of course you do."

"Then you'll tell Chance to back off?"

She makes a noise that's like a groany hum. "I don't know, Arden. Maybe you should wait until you get to know Reese better. I mean, he's a sweetie, but... Chance knows him better than I do. I trust his judgment, and if he thinks it's a bad idea, then it probably is."

"You just said Reese is a sweetie."

"But he has a reputation for being the bang-and-run type. I don't want you to get hurt."

Now it's my turn to groan, though mine is more moany groan than groany hum. "It's my life, Elena. Being a virgin doesn't make me mentally incompetent."

"I know. You're wicked smart, but you're inexperienced when it comes to men. We both know why that is, but like I've told you for years, you can't avoid taking risks forever."

"Which is exactly why I want to sleep with Reese."

"That's not the kind of risk I mean, and you know it." She hesitates yet again, and I can hear her fingernails drumming on some kind of hard surface. "Get to know him. Take these two weeks to become friends with Reese, then decide. You need to try dating, really dating, before you take the next step."

"Says the woman who screwed her fiancé on the night they met."

"I don't want you to regret this, that's all. Besides, you just came back from nine months in South America. At least decompress before you jump in the sack with Reese or anybody."

Decompress? Maybe I do need some downtime, but I'm tired of everyone telling me what to do. My parents never told me what to do, though they offered me advice. My grandmother is another story. Date this guy, don't date that guy. Take this job, don't take that one. Grams is kind of bossy. It's a side effect of her job.

"Have you even told Reese who you are yet?" Elena asks.

"No. I was hoping I wouldn't have to."

"Bite the bullet, Arden."

"Fine," I say with a sigh. "I'll tell him."

I hear a man's voice in the background and know it must be Chance. Elena announces she has to go. We say goodbye, with my promise I won't sleep with Reese until I've at least told him who I am. Where I come from. Why I've stayed a virgin. Elena gave me his cell number, but it takes me an hour to work up the courage to call. When I do, I get his voice mail. I leave a message asking him to please, please, please stop by the apartment so we can talk. I say it's urgent, to make sure he'll show up.

And if he can handle my pedigree, maybe we can get it on tonight.

Problem is, ever since my talk with Elena, I've been starting to think she might be right. Maybe I ought to spend more time with Reese before we hook up. I don't want to wait. Thinking about him makes me ache and burn in all those secret places where no one has ever touched me before. No one but me and my harem of vibrators.

How long do I have to wait? A week? A month? I have no idea what length of time is sufficient before I can hump Reese, the hottie who makes me tingle all over every time he smiles.

Maybe I have gone sex crazy. Elena might be right that I have other reasons for wanting to cross that line with Reese.

So I decide to deal with my lust the way I always have. I change into a billowy nightie, get Rod, and sit on the sofa tucked into the corner with my legs stretched out. Leaning my head back, I picture Reese. His mouth. His eyes. His hot body. I remember how it felt to have my hand on his thigh, so close to his dick. Maybe I won't sleep with him for a while, if ever, but I can use a fantasy of him to help me get some relief.

I picture him naked. All those muscles. His hips undulating while he thrusts into me again and again.

With one hand, I cup my breast through the nightie and pinch the already stiff peak. Oh yes. Reese. Doing that. With his mouth and his teeth. I bend one knee, letting it fall to the side, and slip my hand under my nightie to glide the vibrator up and down my slick cleft. I've watched enough late-night cable to know how it might go if I ever do sleep with my new roommate.

Oh yes, Reese. His expression tense with the need to come. His ragged breaths. His cock filling me with every thrust.

I switch on the vibrator and thrust it inside me the way I imagine Reese doing with his dick. I keep rolling my fingers around my nipple while I work the vibrator, throwing my head back and moaning. I let go of my breast and grip the sofa's back, writhing and gasping while I drive myself closer and closer to climax.

My fantasy keeps going. Reese flipping us over so I'm on top, riding him while he grasps my hips and says dirty things to me.

"Oh yes," I moan. "Yes, Reese, do it like that. Oh God, please, harder, deeper."

I'm almost there. Almost. So close.

Rod needs a little help, so I rub my clit with my other hand while I buck my hips into the thrusts of the vibrator and crank it up so it's buzzing like a giant, crazy bee.

"Oh Reese! Make me come!" My release rocks me like an earthquake, starting with a jolt as my entire body clenches. When the first spasm hits, I shout, "Reese! Yes!"

"Bloody hell."

Though I hear Reese's voice, I think it's in my head, part of the fantasy. With my eyes closed, I keep going while the orgasm pulses through me, keep going until the very last spasm fades. Breathing hard, I open my eyes.

And see Reese standing at the other end of the sofa.

His mouth is gaping. His eyes are wide and kind of wild. He has one hand in his hair, the other at his side where it keeps fisting and loosening. He's staring at me, at the vibrator lodged between my thighs.

I realize I should probably be embarrassed, but all I can think about is how much I want him to take over for Rod. Screw what Elena said. I deserve hot sex with a hot Brit.

"What are you doing?" he says, sounding breathless.

"Giving myself a big O." I turn the vibrator off and grab a tissue to wipe it down. "If you won't do me, I'll do myself."

"But you—" He scrubs that hand in his hair, looking at my face now. "Did you do that because you knew I was on my way over here?"

"How could I know that? I had to leave a message for you."

"Yes, and your message said I should let myself in."

Oh yeah, I had said that. Well, to be fair, at the time when I left the message, I wasn't planning on having a round of solo sex. I also hadn't expected Reese to rush over here so fast.

I stand up. "Are you okay?"

The bulge in his pants is way bigger than usual.

He shoves both hands into his hair, the movement raising his shirt enough that I can see the waistband of his pants.

And the tip of his erection poking out.

Not long ago, maybe an hour before Reese barged into the apartment, I'd been totally on board with Elena's idea that I should wait awhile before getting naked with Reese. Somewhere between getting off on my own and him catching me in the act, I'd jumped overboard. Maybe it's hormones talking. Maybe I should go to my bedroom and shut the door.

But I don't want to.

I love the way Reese is breathing hard, his cheeks are slightly pink, and his cock looks hard enough to crack eggs on it. Not that I'm going to do that. I would love to get my hands on that beefstick, though. And my mouth on it. Suddenly, I forget all the reasons why I should deny myself the thrill of getting it on with the hottest guy I've ever seen who also has the hottest British accent I've ever heard and who makes me hotter than I've ever felt before.

All that wetness dribbling down my inner thighs is because of him.

His chest is still heaving when he lowers his hands and asks, "What did you want to talk about?"

Oh God, I love the rough tone of his voice. Add in his accent, and wow, he could give me a multi-O experience just by reading the phone book to me.

"I was planning to tell you," I say, "that I've changed my mind and we shouldn't have sex."

His face blanks. "Oh."

"But I changed my mind again. I want you inside me, Reese, right now."

"What the—You can't keep changing your mind." He grips the back of his neck, averting his gaze. "I still can't do it, Arden. You're still my almost sister-in-law's best friend, and my brother will still murder me if I touch you."

"Oh please. Why are we letting other people decide what we can and can't do? We're adults. We make up our own minds."

I walk up to him and rub my finger over the red tip of his erection, where it pokes up out of his pants. "I want you, Reese."

"Bloody hell." He grabs my hand before I can run my finger over him again. "This is wrong."

"No, it's not." I guide his hand to my breast, molding it to my body with only the thin nightie separating my skin from his. "It felt so right when I was making myself come while imagining you were inside me. The fantasy of you rocked my world. Now I want the real thing."

He stares at me, mouth open, his tongue sliding across his bottom lip.

I press his hand more firmly to my breast. "Be my first time, Reese. Tonight."

Chapter Seven

Reese

This beautiful, sexy girl is standing in front of me, holding my hand to her tit, asking me to fuck her. I've been propositioned before, several times, but never like this. *Be my first time*, she says. Only once was I a girl's first time, and that was my first time too. I want Arden. Want her like mad. But I keep hearing Chance's voice in my head telling me to be a good little boy and not ruin his fiancée's best friend, the sweet and sort of barmy girl who joined the Peace Corps and who believes in aliens.

But her eyes are pleading with me, and her luscious body is tempting me with all those curves and those breasts, one of which I'm currently fondling. Because she shoved my hand onto it.

Even a monk couldn't stop from getting hard if a woman did that to him. Particularly this woman. And particularly after what I saw her doing a few minutes ago. Honestly, I was hard the second I walked into the flat and found her enjoying one of her sex toys on the sofa.

My mind decides to give me a vivid replay of that moment, of Arden writhing on the sofa while she fucks herself with a vibrator. Was that Rod? Maybe it had been Jack. Christ, I hope it wasn't Big Jim, because I have a feeling a real dick might have a hard time living up to a device that has a name like that.

I'm still having trouble catching my breath. Her tit feels so good, supple and warm with the nipple stiff and pushing against my palm. She smells like sex, because she was giving herself a jolly good time a few minutes ago. The scent of it, musky and sweet, is eroding my willpower much too fast.

"Arden," I say, trying to be mature and levelheaded about it, "I'm not sure we should do this. Chance and Elena—"

"They don't run my life, or yours." She massages the back of my hand, the one wrapped around her breast. "I've waited long enough. You're nice, even if you are British, and you're so damn sexy. I want you, but if you don't want me…"

"Of course I want you." I realize what she said a moment ago and ask, "Why did you say 'even if you are British'?"

"Well, to be honest, when I think of British people, I picture the queen. She's, like, a thousand years old."

"Do I look like the queen?"

Her gaze slides up and down my body, then settles on my cock. She bites her lip. "No, you don't look anything like that."

If she doesn't stop staring at my erection, I can't be held responsible for what I do.

Leave her alone, Reese. It's Chance's voice again, repeating the words he said to me this morning. *Don't do it. Keep your randy paws off Arden.*

Right. The same way Chance kept his randy paws off Elena on the night they met. He told me about that, but he probably wishes he hadn't. I can use it as an excuse to strip Arden naked.

I shouldn't, but I want to. The need pounds inside me, like an alien creature has crawled into my body and demands I feed it Arden's pleasure.

Maybe I've spent too much time around her. An alien? *Get a grip, man.*

Lusting after Arden Clover Pesti might be wrong, but suddenly, I can't think of a single reason why I shouldn't take her up on that offer. After all, I'm the Dixon brother who does the wrong thing the right way.

One more time, for the last time, I ask, "Are you sure you want to do this?"

"Yes, Reese, I'm sure."

"And you haven't been drinking or smoking anything?"

"None of the above. Clean and sober and on fire for you."

I pick her up and carry her into a bedroom, not really noticing or caring whose bedroom it is. It turns out to be Arden's. I set her down on her feet near the bed. The pink bed. Since I know this used to be Kyle Linwood's room, I'm sure he didn't put the pink sheets and fuzzy pink blanket on the bed. Stuffed animals are lined up along the headboard, on top of the pillows.

"Does my girlie room bother you?" Arden asks. "I had my parents mail me some of my stuff, from my apartment back home."

"It doesn't bother me. I've been in worse girlie rooms."

Arden marches up to the headboard, stretches her arm halfway across the bed, which is as far as she can reach, and sweeps the stuffed animals off it. I watch as she crawls across the bed and shoves the rest of them onto the floor. When she climbs off the bed, her nightie rides up and reveals the round cheeks of her arse.

She sashays up to me, tipping her head back to meet my gaze. "How do we start?"

"By getting naked, Luscious."

"Duh. Right." She whips her nightie off over her head and flings it away. "How's that?"

I choke on whatever I'd been about to say, the words having flown straight out of my head. Arden is gorgeous, from her deliciously round tits to her deliciously round arse and those delicious little nipples that poke out at me like they're begging to be tasted. I pore my gaze over her, following her breasts down to her flat belly, and lower to the curly hairs that mark the spot where I want to have my head—between those creamy thighs, with my face buried in those hairs while I feast on her.

"Why aren't you naked yet?" she asks, not sounding bossy, just seeming confused by the fact I'm standing here like a bloody moron.

"Sorry, Luscious. Your beautiful body had me distracted."

I tear my clothes off and ditch them on the floor. My dick is flying at full staff now, waving at Arden like it can't wait to get inside her. I can't wait. It's been years since I got this excited about being with a girl, but something about Arden makes me want her so badly I swear I can already taste her on my tongue.

She bites her lip again.

And that does me in.

I grasp a handful of the covers and yank them off, leaving only the bottom sheet and the pillows on the bed.

Arden giggles.

Her breasts jiggle.

I pick her up and drop her onto the bed. She bounces a little, which makes her tits jiggle again.

"You are so gorgeous," I say while I crawl across the bed to straddle her. "Hands down the sexiest woman I've ever seen."

She smiles shyly.

Now she's shy? Not when she'd shoved my hand on her breast. Not when she'd asked me to be her first time. Definitely not when she stripped off her nightie. But now, when I'm about to take her body, suddenly she's acting shy.

And I love it. She's so thoroughly… disarming.

"You can still change your mind," I hear myself saying, though I can't believe I'm saying it.

She shakes her head. "Not changing my mind."

Crouched on all fours over her body, I dip my head to kiss her. She slips her tongue between my lips, a tentative exploration, and when I curl my tongue around hers, she dives deep. I kiss her slowly, taking my time to heighten her desire and get her ready for me. Of course, she's made herself ready with her little friend on the sofa. Mine won't be the first rod she's taken into her body, but I will be the first actual human to feel her wrapped around me.

Just thinking about that makes me so hungry for her I can hardly breathe.

Well, I might also have trouble breathing because she's devouring me like she wants to taste the back of my throat. I love her enthusiasm, but I have better plans for her.

I give up her mouth and bend my arms so I can reach her tits. Her nipples stick straight up like tiny signposts guiding me to where I want to be, and I tease one of those peaks with my tongue, flicking it side to side, then up and down, until she starts to breathe more heavily. Her mouth opens and closes, over and over, while I tug her rigid peak into my mouth and suckle it.

"Oh that's good," she moans.

The sultry tone of her voice fires a bolt of lust straight into my cock. I need to hurry if I'm going to last until I've got her melting for me, so I kiss and lick a path down her belly, crawling backward at the same time. I can smell her cream even more now, the scent of it intoxicating me and overpowering my senses—and my good sense. I want to thrust inside her right now. But I won't. This is her first time, and a vibrator isn't the same as a real man.

When I reach her mound, I bury my face in all those curly hairs and suck in a deep draft of her feminine scent. Fuck, it's incredible. She moans, and I comb my fingers through those hairs, all the way down to her opening.

"Reese," she breathes, "please hurry. I've waited so long..."

She's already wet—drenched, actually—so maybe I don't need to take as much time as usual. But I never, never skimp on the foreplay. What kind of first time would that be? She deserves everything.

I part her folds with two fingers, intending to get down to it, but I can't resist taking a moment to admire her body. All that beautiful, rosy flesh glistening with the proof of her desire for me. Or maybe that's for Rod.

Why I ask, I can't say for sure. But I glance up at her and say, "What were you thinking about when you had that vibrator inside you?"

She reaches down to ruffle my hair with her fingertips. "You, Reese. I was thinking about you the entire time. You're the reason I got so turned on that I needed to relieve the pressure."

"You do realize an actual man is different from a mechanical device. For one thing, I don't vibrate." I smirk. "Usually."

"Ha-ha. I know a man is different. I might be kooky, but I'm not stupid."

"I know. Just wanted to make sure you don't have... impossible expectations."

She raises her brows and gives me a teasing smile. "Are you going to do me sometime this year? Or do I need to break out Big Jim to get the job done?"

"Is that a challenge?"

"Totally."

"Well, in that case..."

I suck her clit into my mouth and keep sucking hard until a sharp cry erupts out of her and she half whimpers, half shouts, "Yes, Reese, yes!" I take her taut nub between my teeth and tug, then swirl my tongue around it until her breathing turns into staccato panting.

"Oh God," she moans. "I'm about to—"

That's when I stop. I pull my mouth away and lick the flavor of her off my lips. "That's good enough, right? You can suck me off, and we're done."

She gapes at me, her cheeks speckled with pink and her breasts heaving. "What? I—What?"

"Relax, I'm joking."

Her eyes roll upward. She shuts her lids and shakes her head. "You are such a dick."

"No, I have a dick. There's a difference, Luscious." I move her thighs further apart, giving myself another moment to appreciate her rosy flesh that's swollen and slick, the perfect cradle for my cock. Then I realize something. "Shit. I forgot the condom."

Arden makes a sound I can best describe as complete frustration mixed with sheer lust. "You didn't bring one? What kind of man-whore are you? I would've thought you'd always have one on you."

"I do." Patting her thigh, I slide off the bed to find my trousers. Once I've retrieved the condom from the hip pocket, I climb back onto the bed to straddle her again. I wave the condom packet at her. "See? I'm a respectable man-whore after all."

"Oh thank God," she whimpers. "I want you, not Big Jim."

"Glad to hear I rank higher than your sex toy." I get the condom on and kneel between her thighs, encouraging her to bend her knees. "Are you ready?"

"Yes, you asshole, I've been ready forever and ever."

Though I try not to, I can't stop the chuckle that spills out of me. "You're even sexier when you're frustrated. But I hope you'll have something nicer to say than 'asshole' when I'm done."

Before she can say anything else, I push inside her.

Chapter Eight

Arden

Oh. My. God. This feels so incredibly, unbelievably, mind-blowingly amazing. Reese slides into me inch by inch, taking time to let me adjust every step of the way. He looked big, but now that I'm feeling all of him, the only thing I can say is wow. His cock is thick and firm and hot. He glides inside me, lubricated by my body and how outrageously wet I am for him.

Partway in, he pauses. "Is this all right? Does it hurt?"

"No, it feels good. Really good."

"What about now?" He pushes a little harder, but only goes in a tiny bit deeper. "Does that hurt?"

I suddenly realize what he must be worried about. "Don't worry. I broke that silly hymen a long time ago."

His brows shoot up. "You did? With what, Big Jim?"

"No, that was before I had a vibrator. I used the handle of a hairbrush."

"Why would you do that?"

"To get off." I tighten my muscles around him, making him suck in a breath. "Don't stop, please. I'm fine, and I need more of you. So shove that big, gorgeous dick in there harder."

He splutters, like he's about to either laugh or choke, or maybe both.

But he does it. He pulls out until only the head of his cock grazes my entrance, then he thrusts into me with one long, firm, powerful stroke. It's so good, so perfect, so much better than I even imagined. He fills me, consumes me, touches part of me no one and nothing, not even Big Jim, has touched before. Yeah, it's a little uncomfortable at first. I'm not used to having something so big inside me, but I get used to it quickly. And I love it.

"You feel so awesome," I say, desperate to touch him, but I can't. He's kneeling between my legs, holding my thighs while he thrusts in and out, in and out. "That's it, just like that. I love the way you fill me up. Don't stop. I want to feel you come inside me."

He groans deeply, his eyes sliding shut, the look on his face evincing pure pleasure, like I'm the best thing he's ever felt. "Ah, Arden. You're so tight and hot and slick." His whole face scrunches up. "I want to feel you come all over my cock."

"I will. I'm going to. I—" A cry disrupts my words as I clutch the pillow under my head and lift my hips in my desperate need to take him as far inside as humanly possible. A climax builds within me, like a tsunami rolling across the ocean, getting higher and higher the closer it barrels toward the shore. I know I'll come soon, any second, and I can't wait to feel that happen while he's driving into me. "Yes, Reese, more. Harder. Faster. Please, I need you to—"

He growls—swear to God he does, like a ravenous animal—then plants his hands on the bed at either side of me and lunges into me so hard and so deep and so fast that I can't hold back anymore. That tsunami crashes through me while I scream his name and lash all my limbs around him, my body milking him so fiercely I wonder if I'm hurting him. Oh shit, this is better than I imagined, better than I could ever have hoped.

Reese lets out a deep, throaty roar and plows into me with the hardest thrust ever. Then he freezes and shouts. I feel him pulsing, then he backs out and plows into me again, harder, his face wrenched with pleasure-pain. I feel him pulse again as he calls out my name in a strangled shout.

We're both gasping for breath.

He drops onto the bed beside me, landing on his back.

Neither of us speaks for a minute. I can't speak for sure, and I'm betting he feels the same way. Breathless. Awestruck. So completely satisfied that there's no word for it in any language on earth.

"Wow," I say when I can finally speak. "Wow. I mean… wow, Reese, wow."

He laughs softly. "Would you like to say 'wow' a few more times? To make sure I heard you. I may have gone blind and deaf from what we did."

"If you know I said 'wow,' you're not deaf." I wave a hand in his face. "Can you see that?"

"Yes, I see it." He grabs my hand and thrusts my middle finger into his mouth, releasing it little by little. "And I taste it."

His voice gets lower and sexier when he says that, and it makes my clit throb.

I don't know if I can survive another orgasm right now, so I tell him, "Please stop sounding all hot and hungry like that. It's making me horny again."

"And that's a bad thing?" He rolls onto his side to face me and feathers his lips over mine. "You are not only the sexiest woman I've ever seen. You're also hands down the best shag I've ever had."

"But I'm a virgin."

"Not anymore." He lays a hand over my mound, those long fingers curving over it, down between my thighs. "This belongs to me now. Finders keepers and all that bollocks."

"My vagina is not your property." I flip onto my side, gazing into his eyes. "But you can have a lease with option to buy."

He screws up his mouth, averting his gaze. "I'm not the sort who buys anything, not even a car."

"I wasn't begging you to marry me, Reese. It was a joke, that's all."

He lays back on the bed and rubs a hand over his eyes. "Maybe I've made a big mistake by taking your virginity. Naturally, you'll think of me as… someone special, or something."

"No, I won't. Promise." But I do feel kind of connected to him, which is dumb since I've known him for a smidge more than twenty-four hours. Still, that soft, glowy feeling in my chest is spreading into my tummy, and I think I might be in trouble. But I tell him, "Don't worry. I won't get all attached to you and cyber-stalk your fine ass after you go home to England."

"Hmm." Reese lifts his arm, a clear invitation to cuddle up, so I do. He folds his arm around me, his fingers caressing my skin.

"I like you, Arden, and this was bloody fantastic. But nobody can know what we've done. Chance and Elena wouldn't like it."

"Yeah, I guess you're right. Hurting them would suck, and it's not worth it since neither of us wants more than sex. And we're done with that."

I say the words—and intellectually, I mean them—but that glowy sensation won't leave me alone. Maybe it's the afterglow of a monumental orgasm. Maybe in a few hours, it'll go away. I don't want a relationship. All I wanted was to cross that finish line, and I've done it. Reese did it, actually. And holy wow, did he ever do a spectacular job.

"Good, we're agreed," he says, still holding me close. "One amazing night, and it's over."

"Yes. It's over." I paint tiny patterns on his chest with my finger. "Unless we do it one more time. Which, you know, would really be part of the same night."

"Right. I haven't fully inducted you into the world of earth-shattering sex yet, have I?"

"Mm-mm. Better get back to it."

He rolls me over so he's on top of my body and grins. "Are you ready to come even harder?"

I grin too. "Oh yes, please."

Chapter Nine

Reese

I wake up in the morning and realize I'm lying in Arden's bed. I'd meant to sneak out after she fell asleep. First, I'd meant to kiss her good night and casually walk out and go to my room. But she was so sweet and warm tucked under my arm, with her head on my chest, that I couldn't make myself tell her to move. Once she fell asleep, I kept lying there listening to her breathing and inhaling the scent of her, while she still had her head on my chest.

Eventually, I fell asleep.

Which explains why I'm in her bed, but not why I couldn't bring myself to leave her last night. I never spend the night with a woman, not anymore. The few times I did, the girl would get clingy and needy the next morning, and I had to be an arse and sneak out when she wasn't looking. Trust me, telling a woman you don't really want to date her, that having sex doesn't mean you're signing on for a lifetime commitment, never works. So yes, I skulked out.

But not last night. And not this morning.

I'm lying here in Arden's pink bed, but she isn't in it.

Have I been sneaked out on like I'd done to women in the past? Maybe it's my punishment for behaving like a "sleazoid." I'd only done that three times, and not in at least four years. Chance had given me a dressing-down for that behavior when he found out what I'd done, and believe me, there's nothing like a big-brother lecture to make a bloke never want to go through it again.

Besides, I never liked letting my family down.

Which sounds odd, I know. I'm the brother who screws around and doesn't stay for breakfast, but I also don't run off without saying goodbye. Not anymore. Not after seeing the disappointed look on Chance's face. He hadn't told our parents what I'd done, but his disappointment was more than enough.

I turn on my side in Arden's bed and get an exhilarating dose of her scent. Not only the aroma of sex from the three times we'd done it. The scent of her. I crush her pillow to my face and haul in an even bigger dose of her. The aroma fills my nostrils and overpowers my senses, making me feel strangely… relaxed.

Ah, the scent of Arden.

What am I doing? I spring up, sitting there with her pillow in my hands, and try to answer my own question. I can't be… enjoying this. Being in her bed. Waking up here. Spending the night with her.

No. I'm still sleepy, that's all.

I drop her pillow and get out of the bed, gathering my clothes and pulling them on while employing every fragment of my tattered willpower to keep from thinking about how fantastic her pillow smells.

Other aromas waft into the bedroom now. Is that bacon? Pancakes? I sniff the air, and my stomach grumbles.

Maybe Arden hasn't skulked away from me while I slept. In her bed. The pink one.

I tiptoe out into the hallway and down to the living room, like I'm a prowler about to get caught. Arden is in the kitchen, cooking something that sizzles on a skillet and humming softly to the music playing through her earbuds. I can't hear the music, but I recognize the tune as one of those power ballads from the eighties. The bar blocks my view of the lower half of her body, but I can see her shirt. The pastel plaid fabric looks so good on her, and she's left the shirt half unbuttoned so I can see the center of her chest and get a tempting glimpse of the sides of her breasts.

Why couldn't she have worn a turtleneck? Is that too much to ask for?

She looks up, sees me, and smiles as she takes her earbuds out. "Good morning, Reese. Hungry?"

That smile. It's the single most beautiful thing I've ever seen, full of bright, sunshiny joy.

Christ, I've turned into one of those lovey-dovey idiots.

"Good morning, Arden," I say. "I'm starved. Is that pancakes I smell?"

"Mm-hm. Blueberry this morning. I hope you like that."

"I'll eat anything. Just ask my family. Dane once dared me to eat a handful of grasshoppers, and I did it."

"Ew." She wrinkles her nose. "I don't cook insects for breakfast. Only for Thanksgiving dinner."

"Is that an American tradition?" I ask, taking a seat at the bar. "I thought it was turkey and pumpkin pie, but insects sounds a lot more interesting."

She aims her spatula at me. "You do realize I was kidding, right? I never touch insects, much less eat them. They're icky."

"Afraid of grasshoppers? Don't worry, I'll protect you from them." I pat my chest with both hands. "I'm your personal insect repellent."

Her snort transforms into a sputtering laugh. "That's even ickier. You're a walking bottle of chemical spray? Not sexy."

"Sorry. No more talk of creepy-crawlies, I promise."

"Good. Because I saw bugs the size of buses down in Ecuador." She flips a pancake, and only half of it lands on the griddle. She scoops up the half that's hanging off the side and tries to get it all on the cooking surface, but it winds up wrinkled. "Ugh. I'll eat that one."

"You're still doing better than I would. My mum won't let me near uncooked food anymore, not since I tried to poach an egg in the microwave and it exploded."

"How do you make an egg explode?"

"By cooking it with the shell on."

Arden smiles with her lips sealed, and it's the sweetest expression I've ever seen. "Guess you win the worst chef award."

"Don't I also win the wow award for most incredible taking of virginity?"

Her sweet little smile broadens into a grin. "Yep, you win that one for sure."

For some reason, I feel the need to add, "We can't do that again."

Her grin fades, but only for a few seconds, then that lips-sealed smile returns. This time, it carves out divots in her cheeks, like she has a brilliant secret that she's not going to share.

"What are you plotting, Arden?"

"Oh, nothing." She flips another pancake, this time getting all of it on the griddle, her head down but her eyes turned up to look at me. "Just imagining how I can seduce you."

"No, Arden." I try to sound stern, but I'm bloody awful at it. Resistance is not my strong suit, remember? "We can't do that anymore."

Even I don't believe me.

But dammit, I will try to not fuck her. Honestly, I'll try.

No, I won't try. I absolutely will *not* have sex with Arden. Never again. End of story.

She laughs, and her eyes sparkle.

"You think my resolve is funny?" I say.

"No, I think it's cute that you think you, a total player, can keep saying no when a woman wants you so bad she'll do anything to get you naked again."

Luckily, she finishes making the pancakes before I can think of anything to say in response. She wants to eat on the sofa, but I insist we have our breakfast at the bar.

Arden leans across the bar to set our plates there, making her half-unbuttoned shirt fall away from her body. I can see even more of her breasts.

My mouth waters, and not from the savory food she's placed in front of me.

She ambles around the bar to where the stools and I are waiting for her. The barmy girl whose shirt is half open is wearing nothing else but those plaid knickers I'd seen on the night we met.

"Why aren't you dressed?" I ask, and I almost cringe at the humiliating, panicked tone of my voice.

"I am dressed," she tells me. "Not ready for public viewing yet, but dressed."

And I can't think of anything to say to that.

Of course, she perches on the stool right next to mine. When I move to the next one over, she moves over too. The girl is relentless. I can't possibly be *that* good in bed. I mean, I'm good. But not so fantastic that women can't bear to not fuck me. Her insistence must be strictly because she was a virgin. I'm all she knows, about sex, so naturally she thinks I'm the most incredible lover on the planet.

Being around her might give me an ego the size of Australia.

I have no choice but to sit there with her inches away, the intoxicating scent of her more powerful than the smell of the pancakes and bacon. My willpower, which I'd thought—or maybe prayed—had reassembled itself, is getting new cracks. I'm only a man, not a robot with no feelings and no dick. Mine, by the way, is awake and ready for action. I really hope Arden doesn't peek under the bar and see that. The woman does not need more ammunition for blowing holes in my self-control.

She wriggles her bum on her stool while humming with pleasure as she chews a bite of bacon.

Never in my life have I needed my willpower so much, and it's failing me at every turn. Am I a complete and total arsehole? I'm starting to think the answer is yes.

"Let's go for a walk," I say. I'm done eating, since unfulfilled lust apparently makes me as ravenous as a starved lion who's caught a tasty gazelle. "It looks like a beautiful day out there."

"It is." She slips a forkful of pancake between her lips, and syrup dribbles down those lips and onto her chin, a single drop of it threatening to fall off. "But I was thinking we should go to the zoo."

"The zoo?" I say the words, but I'm not actually listening to her. That drop of syrup has captured all of my attention, because if it drips off her chin, it will land on one of those gorgeous tits.

While I stare at her chin and half pray for, half curse at the possibility of the syrup splashing onto her breast, she launches into a description of everything that's "awesome and so ridiculously fun" about the zoo. When she starts rambling on about museums, even that doesn't catch my attention. That drop of syrup is still hanging there, like it's frozen in place.

I'm five seconds away from licking it off.

Arden grabs a napkin and wipes her mouth and chin.

Something like disappointment ripples through me. Maybe later, I'll get the syrup and drizzle it over her naked body so I can lick off every last molecule of it.

No, you will not do that, you raging arsehole.

I volunteer to wash the dishes while Arden gets dressed. Actually dressed this time. She comes out of her bedroom wearing jeans, a loose-fitting shirt that falls below her hips, and sandals that show off her adorable toes and the neon-green nail polish on them.

"Let's go," she says. "You're a New York virgin, and I'm going to show you all the most fabulous places in the city."

"Sounds like fun." The zoo and museums don't appeal to me that much, but I love listening to her talk about… anything. "But as a reminder, there will be no sex."

I can't say for sure which of us I'm reminding.

Arden smiles, sexily, and takes my hand. "Don't you trust me, Reese?"

Not with my willpower. Absolutely not.

But I let her lead me out of the apartment, with my hand wrapped around her smaller one, and try not to think about how good she looks in her oversize shirt.

Christ, every last thing about her turns me on.

I'm absolutely doomed.

Chapter Ten

Arden

Reese hadn't been thrilled about going to the zoo or museums, but he gets really into it once we're there. I haven't done anything this fun in a long time, since way before I went to Ecuador. I love to have a good time, but my family history can make that difficult. When I mumble something like that to Reese, thinking he won't hear me, he does hear it.

"Don't you get along with your family?" he asks.

"Of course I do. They're amazing, I love them."

"What's the problem? Why does your family keep you from having a good time?"

Reese and I are in the butterfly garden, so I focus on the beautiful critters flitting around in here when I say, "It's nothing they do. It's the fact of who we are."

"I don't understand."

How could he? Everyone in New York knows my family, or at least my grandmother, but Reese isn't from here. I don't know how to start, so I go with the blunt approach.

"My grandmother is Celeste Arnaud."

Once I announce that, most people get it right away. Reese doesn't. He stares at me like I've babbled in another language.

"She's the founder of Bonsoir Beauty Inc.," I tell him. "The second-largest cosmetics company in the world."

"Oh." His brows crinkle with the cutest confusion. "I'm a man. Why would I know what you're talking about?"

"Because my grandmother is famous. Bonsoir is huge, and she's an icon."

He glances at a big orange butterfly, shoves his hands in his pants pockets, and sighs. "Afraid I've never heard of her. She's your mother's mother, right? Her last name is different, so I assume—"

"Nope. Grams kept her maiden name when she married Granddad because her company was already making a name for itself. She's also very proud of her French heritage. She's American, though. No accent."

"She's your father's mother, then."

"That's right. My dad is Marcel Pesti. My mom's name is Tally."

He watches me with a strange expression for a few seconds, then asks the question he's obviously been working up the nerve to ask. "I know it's a cheeky question, but how rich is your grandmother?"

"She's the number three female billionaire in the world. There are over two hundred of them, you know."

"No, I didn't know that." He scrunches his lips and hunches his shoulders. "Your grandmother is a billionaire?"

"Yeah, but she's not super stuffy or anything. Grams is pretty cool, when she's not butting into my life."

His mouth opens, but he seems incapable of speaking.

Yeah, talking about my grandmother often has that effect on people.

Desperate for something to say to break the tension, I announce out of absolutely nowhere, "I don't have any brothers or sisters."

At least his blank expression has disappeared.

He seems genuinely interested when he asks, "None at all? I can't imagine not having brothers."

"You guys are close, aren't you?"

"Always have been. Chance, as the oldest, thinks it's his job to keep the rest of us in line. Dane is the intellectual, the one who invents things. I'm the youngest, and the biggest disappointment."

"You are not a disappointment."

"If you knew me, you wouldn't say that."

"Does your family say that?"

"No. They're always supportive." He scrunches his mouth up again. "Well, except for one time. When Chance found out I'd shagged a girl and run away while she was asleep, he gave me a lecture about respecting women. The girl in question was best friends with Chance's girlfriend, so that's how he found out."

"You don't run out on women anymore."

"No. I did that three times, but never again after my brother's lecture." Reese glances at me, his mouth twisted into a wryly crooked smile. "Chance will call me an arsehole and a complete fuck-up when he finds out what I've done to you."

"You haven't done anything to me. We did it together." I move closer, leaning into him. "From what Elena says about Chance, he would never call you anything nasty."

Reese leans into me. "You're right. I'm feeling sorry for myself, that's all."

"Because you slept with me after promising not to."

"Not only that. I also lost my job."

I slip my hand into his big palm, threading my fingers through his, and rest my cheek on his arm. "What happened?"

"Does it matter?"

"Maybe it's not my business, but I'd like to know."

He closes his fingers around my hand. "I was a copywriter at an advertising agency, but I was made redundant three weeks ago."

"Redundant?"

"It means I was let go. 'Laid off' I think is what Americans call it."

"That's awful. What will you do now?"

He shrugs. "I'm getting redundancy pay, but I need to find a new job. I probably shouldn't have come here for a holiday instead of searching for a new position, but I needed… I don't know. A break."

"That's understandable. I'm sure your family gets it."

Reese squirms, his face pinching into a tight expression. "I haven't told them yet. They think I took time off from work."

"Why haven't you told them about getting laid off?"

"It's humiliating. Chance is a successful lawyer, even has his own firm now with Elena. Dane is successful too, has his own company, which leaves me as the unemployed loser in the family."

"No one would say that." I turn toward him, still holding his hand. "Getting made redundant doesn't mean you're a loser. It happens to a lot of people."

He angles toward me and studies me for a moment. "What about you? What's your profession? If you're from a wealthy family, do you even need to work?"

Though I would completely understand it if he were envious of my family and my life, he doesn't sound like that at all. He seems curious, not irritated.

Starting with the less shocking truth seems like the best plan. "I'm a freelance fact checker."

"Fact checker? What does that mean?"

"Authors and publishers hire me to make sure they got the facts straight in the stuff they publish, which means I do a lot of research. I specialize in science topics."

"I guess that shouldn't surprise me, since you're very clever." He gives me a playful smile. "Even if you are barmy."

"You should know by now that I'm not sensitive about how weird I am. I like being kooky."

"And you should be proud of your barmy nature. It's endearing." He pauses, glancing down at the ground, then looks at me again. "You didn't answer the other question. Do you need to work, or do you just like to?"

I want to tell him the truth, but that's never worked out well for me. Over the years, I've used the truth as a means of testing guys to find out if they're really interested in me or if they like the prestige of dating Celeste Arnaud's granddaughter. Ninety-nine percent of them fail the first test—my kooky behavior. Their eyes light up when I tell them the part hardly anyone knows about. And ninety-nine percent of the one percent who pass the first test will fail the second one.

Reese is different. I feel it. He passed my kookiness test, and after a couple days with him, I get the sense he might pass the other test. Do I want him to? He lives in another country, and we're such opposites.

What have I got to lose? I gave this man my virginity, so maybe I should go ahead and tell him everything.

"Did I push too far?" he asks.

"No, not at all." I take a deep breath and dive in. "Grams set up a trust fund for me when I was born. On my eighteenth birthday, I started receiving a monthly stipend that more than covers anything I might need or want. I can request more if I have an emergency or something. When my grandmother dies, I'll get the whole enchilada. I hope that doesn't happen for a long, long time."

Reese seems to be waiting for me to go on.

I suck in a breath and blurt out the rest. "My trust fund is five hundred million dollars."

His jaw drops. He keeps hold of my hand, but he doesn't move or speak for several seconds. "Five hundred million?"

I nod, biting my lip. "Grams is very generous."

"Well, that's bloody fantastic for you."

He's smiling, like he means that.

"You're not, like, disgusted?" I ask. "Or seeing dollar signs floating in front of your eyes? You don't feel the urge to ask me to marry you?"

"No," he says, laughing. "I don't do relationships, Arden, I told you that. But I'm glad you don't need to worry about money. It's awful having to think about that all the time."

"Chance has a lot of money, right?"

"He does, and I'm happy for him too."

"Not being well off doesn't make you a loser or a disappointment."

He lets go of my hand to scratch his chin. "I know that, but knowing it and feeling it are different things."

"You can have half my money if you want."

He chuckles at my offer. "That's generous, but no thank you. I don't know you well enough to accept a gift like that, and I wouldn't accept it even if we did know each other well. It's too much."

"You mean that, don't you?"

"I do."

I clasp his hand again and lead him away from the butterfly garden. "Tell me about your brother Dane. You said he invents things."

"Let's not talk about Dane right now."

"Why not? Does he make nuclear weapons for terrorists?"

Reese chuckles. "No, love, he doesn't work for terrorists. He started his own company a few years ago, to sell the devices he designs."

We pass the gorilla exhibit, but I keep us headed down the path because I have a destination in mind. And an activity in mind. He'll say no, but I'm determined to have my way. Reese doesn't seem like he can say no for long, which means I'll get what I want.

Him. His body. His incredible dick.

Maybe I'm going a little crazy with the "shagging," as Reese calls it, because I was a virgin until last night. But no, I'm sure it's more than that. It's him. Reese Dixon is so… lovable. Getting to know him a little better makes me want him even more.

"What kind of devices?" I ask.

"Devices? Oh, you mean the bits and bobs Dane makes." Reese grumbles, and if he's saying words, I can't understand them. Finally, he says, "My brother designs, manufactures, and sells sexual wellness devices."

I stop, bringing Reese to a halt with me. "Sexual wellness?"

Reese bows his head. "Dane makes sex toys. Vibrators. Dildos. Anything that helps women satisfy their needs."

"Only for women? He doesn't make things for men?"

"No. Only women." Reese's mouth jacks up at one corner. "As you can imagine, Dane is very, very popular with the ladies."

"Making sex toys doesn't mean he's great in bed." I seize a handful of Reese's shirt and drag him closer. "Nobody does it better than you."

"I appreciate the compliment, but I'm the only man you've been with."

"Maybe I should do your brothers, so I have something to compare you to."

"That's not funny." He slides an arm around my waist. "I'd love to do you right here in the zoo, on the main path, but we'd both get arrested for that."

I put my arms around him and raise onto my tippy toes, intending to kiss him.

He pushes me away and stumbles backward a few steps. "No, Arden, we're not doing that anymore."

"Who knew hot sex would make you so uptight?"

"I am not uptight. I'm trying to do the right thing, which I admit is a bit of a stretch for me. But I'm giving it a go, and your constant attempts to break my willpower aren't helping."

Am I being a total slut? If I am, it's kind of his fault for being so great at sex. Still, I don't want to scare him away. "I'm sorry. You're being so nice, and I'm acting like a crazy person. I promise to stop trying to seduce you."

"That would be helpful."

Guess I have to nix my plan to drag him into a secluded, shady spot and beg him to corrupt me some more. Well, let's say I'm pressing pause on that plan.

I turn and wave for him to follow me. "Come on. We've got plenty more places to see."

Chapter Eleven

Reese

Arden tows me down various paths until we exit the zoo. She stops us outside the entrance and smiles so brightly it gives me a different sort of warm feeling, the kind that makes me want to hug her instead of doing dirty things to her.

"Should we go to the aquarium or museums first?" she asks.

Her excitement about zoos and museums makes me like her even more. I know she loves science—she told me she specializes in that subject in her fact-checking job—and I want to see how excited she'll get about it. "Museums first."

"Awesome. I love museums even more than the zoo. Should we start with history or science?"

"Your choice."

She grabs my hand again and leads me away. "Science it is."

A taxi takes us to our destination, and now we're inside the New York Hall of Science surrounded by children and their parents. I don't see any other adults without children, only me and Arden.

"Is this a children's museum?" I ask.

"Technically, I guess. But the exhibits are fantastic." She eyes me sideways, her hand clamped around mine and her lips curling up in a teasing way. "I know you're a naughty boy, but surely you know how to have innocent fun too."

Christ, I wish she wouldn't say things like that. Or look at me that way. Or… exist. Nothing short of annihilating her from history seems likely to keep my cock at bay.

I let her guide me through the museum and can't help smiling every time she gets excited about something, anything, everything. I've never met anyone as happy as Arden. She takes pleasure in the simplest things, from a display of orange pink flagging tape that hangs above our heads to an exhibit about health and human evolution. Arden insists I pose next to the articulated human skeleton on display there so she can take a picture. Then she asks me to take a picture of her posing with the skeleton. Finally, she has us both pose with it while she takes a selfie of us.

Strangely, it's the most fun I've had in ages.

Next, she takes me to the American Museum of Natural History. I love watching her enjoy these places. She's so alive and engaged, excited by every little thing even though she tells me she's visited these museums many times. I've gone to museums with my parents when I was younger, but I never had such a good time doing it. My parents are plenty of fun, but no one on earth relishes life the way Arden does.

She insists we buy tickets for the Hayden Planetarium, which has some sort of show about alien planets. I let her decide where we sit once we're inside, and she chooses seats in the third row because, she assures me, "it's the absolute best place to see everything and feel like you're right in the middle of it all." We're very close to the giant black ball that she tells me is the projector for the movie-like show.

"Will your grey alien friends pop out of the projector?" I ask.

"No, they're way too covert to do something like that."

Lately, I've gotten to know her playful looks, and she's giving me one of them right now.

I smirk and say, "I'm sure you've been to these alien worlds we're about to see."

"Oh yeah, loads of times. I'm a frequent flyer on the ET Express."

The room goes dark as the show begins. Arden holds my hand throughout it, and we both lean our heads back to take in the experience. I find myself ignoring the film projected above our heads and instead watching Arden. The delight and wonder on her face captivates me, and rather than thinking about sex, I imagine walking through the park with her again, or having dinner with her, or… doing all sorts of normal, boring things that I know won't seem normal or boring if I'm with her. I realize with a mental jolt what it is I really want.

I want to date her.

We've known each other for a few days, but I want—no, I need more time with her. Time to see more of the world through her eyes. Time to hold her hand like I'm doing right now, and time to hold her in my arms while we talk or watch the telly or… anything.

Chance and Dane will never believe this if I tell them.

After the natural history museum, we go back to the apartment, having had our fill of fun for the day. Arden collapses onto the sofa, pretending to be so exhausted she can't stay awake. She has one leg hooked over the sofa's arm, the other on the coffee table, her arms flung out to the sides, and her eyes closed. She's also fake snoring.

"I'll make dinner," I say. "What are you in the mood for? Grasshoppers on a bed of wild rice?"

She cracks one lid open. "Ha-ha, you're hilarious. Do you even know how to cook rice?"

"I told you about the exploded egg incident."

"Right." She starts to heave herself off the sofa. "I'll make dinner."

"No, you won't." I grasp her shoulders and push her back down. "Relax. I'll figure something out."

And by figuring something out, I mean I'll ring a pizza place and have our dinner delivered right to our door. I even order one of those apple pizzas for dessert. Don't I know how to impress a woman?

We eat on the sofa and talk more in between mouthfuls of cheese-laden food.

"Tell me more about your parents," I say. "You mentioned they're hippies."

"Yep. They own a really cool shop in Stockbridge. That's in Massachusetts, which is right next to New York. The state, not the city. Anyway, Mom and Dad have a New Agey store called the Emerald Eye. Don't ask me why, but that's what my parents decided to call it."

"I thought you were from New York."

"No, I'm from Stockbridge. My grandparents are from New York, and Grams's company is here." Arden consumes a bite of pizza before continuing. "My parents aren't into the whole corporate lifestyle, even though Grams tried to get Dad to take a job at her company. More than once she's tried. Dad always says no. When he married my mom, they moved to Stockbridge. It's a cool, artsy town. That's where Mom's from, and where I was born and raised."

"How did you meet Elena?"

"In college. We both went to Northwestern. That's a university in Illinois." She studies her half-eaten slice of pizza for several seconds, then sets it down on the paper plate on her lap. "I wanted to see a new place, so I decided going away to college was the right option for me."

Eating a couple mouthfuls of pizza gives me a chance to think about what to say next. I want to ask her a million questions, but I don't want to seem like an annoying prick who's poking his nose into her life.

Finally, I settle on a question. "If you're not from New York, how do you know all the museums so well? And the zoo? And all the restaurants?"

"Because I've visited Elena lots. She lived here for years and years."

"Chance has lived in America for a long time, but I never visited him."

"You said once you never 'got round' to it. Why is that?"

I shrug. "Never thought about it. I grew up in the country, just outside one of those chocolate-box villages. I went to uni in London, but that's the extent of my travels, until now."

"What's uni?"

"University."

She sets her plate on the table. "What did you study in college?"

"Business." I give her a wry smile. "I know that sounds odd coming from someone like me, but I always wanted to have a business of my own. Hasn't worked out that way, though."

"What do you mean 'coming from someone like' you?"

"I'm not the serious type, like my brothers. Shagging and playing sports are my favorite pastimes."

"Seems like shagging is Chance's favorite pastime too. Elena says he's completely obsessed with getting her naked and—"

"You stop right there." I hold up a hand to emphasize how much I want her to not talk about my brother's sex life. Chance told me he screwed Elena five minutes after they met, but he didn't give me the graphic details of their elevator encounter. "I don't need or want to know anything about what Chance and Elena do in bed."

"Point taken." She tears off another bite of pizza and speaks with her mouth full. "When are you going to tell me why you're afraid of relationships?"

I open my mouth to deny it, again, but freeze. Ever since Arden first suggested I'm scared of relationships, I've kept thinking about that. Whether she's right. Whether there is a reason behind my behavior. I can't believe I want to talk to her about this, but I suddenly realize I do want that. "Let me start by saying I'm not afraid. But I might be… reluctant."

"Okay. I'll accept 'reluctant' for the moment."

Setting down my paper plate, I rub my hands up and down my thighs. "When I was at school, girls didn't pay much attention to me until I joined the rugby team. I was sort of shy back then. Sports helped me get over that. And when I started scoring the winning goals, girls started propositioning me. I guess I learned that sports and sex go hand in hand, and that women only want me for one thing."

"Hmm. Did your parents know what was going on?"

"Do you think I'm an idiot?" I say. "I learned how to hide things from them. They caught me with a girl in my bedroom once, and I got a stern talking-to. But by then, I liked sex too much to give it up. I got better at hiding what I was up to."

She chews her last mouthful of pizza and swallows before she asks, "Do you still think sex is all you're good for?"

"No. At uni, I realized I'm pretty good at business too, especially marketing and advertising."

"But you still think you don't want a relationship with any woman."

Here, tonight, with Arden… I'm beginning to reevaluate what I want. My realization from earlier today comes back to me, and

I know without any doubts that I want more than sex with this woman.

"Never mind, I'm being too nosy," Arden says. She grabs a fresh paper plate and puts two slices of apple pizza on it. She holds the plate between us. "Time for dessert."

After we eat the apple strudel pizza, we watch two movies on television, then it's time for bed. Arden asks if I want to sleep with her—just sleep, no sex—but I say I'd rather sleep in my own room. It's a lie. I'd much rather crawl into bed with her for the night, but I don't trust my willpower.

I walk her to her bedroom door.

She kisses my cheek.

"There's something I need to tell you," I say.

"Go on."

"I want to date you, Arden."

She stares at me, her gaze nailed to mine. "Date? As in… date?"

"Yes."

"Isn't that kind of what we've been doing all day?"

"Sure, but I want to make it official." I hold out my hand like I want to shake hers, realize that's a stupid thing to do, and clasp her hands instead. "Let's get to know each other for the rest of the two weeks until the wedding. No sex, just dating. Are you interested in that? With me?"

"Of course I am." She smiles shyly, the way she did right before we had sex for the first time. "I'd love to date you, Reese."

"Brilliant." I kiss her forehead. "Good night, Arden."

"Good night."

She goes into her room and shuts the door.

I'm dating. Me. Dating. It's a precursor to a relationship, and I'm volunteering for it.

And it feels bloody fantastic.

Chapter Twelve

Arden

This morning seems brighter and more beautiful than ever before. Reese and I are dating. For the first time ever, I feel like I'm with a guy who doesn't want my trust fund or my body. Well, not only my body. Reese asks about my family and the things I like to do. He lets me drag him through museum after museum and even seems to enjoy it.

I love being with him.

Okay, I've known him for barely more than two days, three counting today which has just begun. I don't love him. But I can love being with him and love the way he makes me feel. Reese is surprisingly sweet, given his reputation as a player. And his determination to not have sex with me only makes me like him even more.

Despite the fact I want to climb all over his naked body.

I've decided to give him the rest of the week for just dating. After that, I want him. If I have to prance around in my undies all day and all night to get his attention, I will do it. Maybe I'll try walking around buck naked in the apartment. He can't resist that, can he?

I climb out of bed, stretch, and yawn, while I think about what Reese and I can do together today. I haven't shown him the art museums yet. Or Central Park. Or Coney Island. Ooooh, so many wonderfully fun places to take him.

Today, we are going to make out. No sex does not mean no kissing, and I'm in desperate need of his lips on mine and his tongue in my mouth.

But I'd really love his tongue somewhere else…

I put on panties and a bra, then by habit I open the bedroom door. I don't like being shut in all the time, and I'm used to living alone. Reese's bedroom door is shut, so I assume he's still sleeping. I start doing tai chi, relaxing into the sequence of gentle, easy movements. The peacefulness of the routine sends all thoughts drifting away, so for once, I'm free of lustful fantasies about the sexy Brit sleeping across the hall.

Out the corner of my eye, I see the door to Reese's bedroom swing open.

And there he is. The reason for my insanely intense lust. Standing there with nothing on but a pair of black briefs. Sure, I've seen him naked and explored every inch of that body, but something about Reese in those tight briefs makes me start to tingle all over in the best way. It feels decadent and naughty.

He saunters across the hall to my room and leans against the doorjamb, tipping his head to the side while he regards me with nonsexual interest. "What are you doing? I don't know much about yoga, but that doesn't look like what you're about right now."

Looking at him makes me lose my concentration, so I give up on finishing my routine. "It's tai chi, which is very relaxing and steadying. Some people call it meditation in motion."

"You meditate?"

I sit down on the bed. "Yeah. Why are you so surprised? Aren't crazy people allowed to seek a higher state of consciousness?"

"Well, yes, of course." He ambles over to the bed and sits down beside me. "I've never seen anyone actually doing meditation or tai chi or anything like it. My family isn't into that sort of thing. Elena has Chance doing yoga, but I think he only goes along with that so he can use it to seduce her. I wouldn't mind watching a sexy girl twist her body into all those yoga poses."

He winks at me.

"Down, boy," I say. "Afraid I don't do yoga."

"We can invent our own version."

He's got that look in his eye, the one that makes me shiver in the most enticing way. But I agreed to celibacy, which was his idea, so he has no call to be looking at me like he wants to tickle my tummy and rip my clothes off.

And he really has no right to be so hot and British.

"You'd better stop talking," I tell him. "Your accent makes me horny, and I'm trying to stick to your no-sex plan. Better put on some baggy pants and a big old sweater too."

His sizzling bod in those black briefs is making my mouth water.

"I didn't bring any clothes like that," he says. "The weather's too warm, love."

"Yeah, but I'm still obsessed with screwing you. Can't help it. You look so damn good in… everything. So it's really your fault I'm obsessed with sex."

"I see." He slants toward me until his shoulder bumps into mine, and his voice goes all deep and sexy. "I can grow a thick beard if that will help."

"That will take too long, and besides, I doubt it would alleviate the problem." I slide my fingers along his jaw, loving the scratchy feel of it. "You're way hotter with morning stubble. A beard would probably turn me into a wild animal."

"But I might like that."

I smack his thigh. "Cut that out. No more flirting until you're ready to get naked with me again. Capisce?"

"All right, have it your way." He gets up and stretches, giving me a fantastic view of his body and the lump in his briefs. "What should we do today?"

"Let's play it by ear." I stand and shoo him away. "Go get dressed, you steamy hunk of man candy."

Reese grabs me, hauls me into that mouthwatering body, and plants a firm but brief kiss on my lips. "Anything you want, Luscious."

Then he saunters back into his room and shuts the door.

We make breakfast together—which, with this guy, means we spend more time laughing and kissing than actually cooking—and afterward we head out to my favorite art museums. It's the start of a week-long adventure consisting of visits to everywhere we can think of that sounds like fun. On day four, we visit Coney Island and have a total blast there. Bumper cars with Reese makes me laugh so hard my eyes water. On the roller coaster, I shriek and cling to Reese. He grins the entire time, keeping his arm around me.

After that, we play games like Whac-A-Mole and Water Racer—and I win a stuffed giraffe, which I give to Reese. He does a formal, courtly bow when he accepts my gift. And of course, he kisses me—though he keeps it PG rated.

I've never had such a good time. Ever.

We go shopping too, and Reese buys me a Cyclone T-shirt to commemorate the day we rode that roller coaster together. I buy him a shirt with a mermaid on it. He promptly whips off the shirt he's been wearing and pulls on the new one, spreading his arms and grinning. I get that glowy sensation in my chest again, like I had the night we did the deed, the one that feels good and weird at the same time. At the aquarium, we watch the sea lions and the fish and all that stuff, but then Reese pulls me into a dark corner and kisses me. It's slow and sensual and not at all in line with his plan for celibate dating. At least, it seems that way to me. I love it anyway. Not only does he have a magic dick, but he's also got a magic mouth.

Reese insists on buying me dinner at a pizza restaurant, which is delish, then we walk along the boardwalk hand in hand while we watch the sun dip lower and lower in the sky. Once it's dark, we head for the Wonder Wheel. I haven't been on a Ferris wheel in ages and ages. When I told Reese that earlier, he insisted we must ride one today. After we climb into a car, he slips his arm around me, and I rest my head on his shoulder. It feels nice and comfortable, like we've known each other for months instead of days.

As soon as the wheel starts moving, Reese nuzzles my cheek and whispers, "I'm not afraid of having a relationship with you."

My breath catches. Dating is one thing, but a relationship would take us to the next level. Is he really prepared for that?

I turn my face toward him, and our eyes meet. "Are you saying what I think you're saying?"

"Depends what you think I'm saying." He drags his fingertips down my cheek. "I want to get involved with you, Arden. Seriously involved."

My voice refuses to work. Stunned speechless? Me? Wow, it's hard to believe.

Reese brushes his thumb over my lips. "Do you want that?"

"A relationship? With you?" I smile. "Yes, I'd love that."

He smiles too, but it's no exuberant grin. It's sweet and tender.

"Don't relationships involve sex?" I ask.

"I, uh, guess so." He bows his head, scratches the back of it, then looks at me again. "But we shouldn't. Not yet."

"Okay, fine, we'll stick to celibacy." I slump on the seat and throw him a sideways glance. "It's not fair to be so irresistible when you refuse to have sex with me."

"I'll make it worth the wait, I promise."

Our car reaches the ground, and we climb out of it.

Reese slings an arm around me. "How about ice cream?"

Yeah, that's what I'm hungry for right now. Ice cream. Sheesh. Maybe if I get to lick it off him…

But we stay platonic for the rest of the evening and go to sleep in our separate rooms.

Damn.

Chapter Thirteen

Reese

Spending this much time with Arden has proved a hard test for my willpower. She's so sexy, even when she's shoving huge bites of pizza into her mouth. To survive a week with her, I've had to put up some walls between us. Real walls. The kind that separate my bedroom from hers.

Why can't I shag her again? I know there was a reason, but it's fading from my memory.

Did I actually tell her I want a relationship? Yeah, I did. And I meant it. Dating seemed like a huge step, but a relationship feels like jumping off the Empire State Building. I love that feeling. It's the best high in the world, next to making love to Arden. Which I can't do. Because I said we shouldn't.

Why did I do that?

I get a reminder the next morning when Chance rings me—to check up on me, naturally. I can't be trusted not to deflower every virgin in New York City.

When I answer my mobile, I speak before Chance can. "No, I'm not having sex with Arden."

"Good day to you too, Reese."

"Don't pretend you aren't ringing me to make sure I've kept my randy paws off your fiancée's best friend."

"Maybe I am, but that's not the only reason I rang you."

I sigh, leaning my head back against the sofa. I've been sitting here while I wait for Arden to wake up and emerge from her room. "What else do you want, Chance?"

"Elena needs Arden in New Hampshire on Wednesday instead of Friday. She needs help with some sort of wedding dress crisis. It sounds like nothing to me, but Elena's having an anxiety attack."

"Aren't you loving all the feminine bollocks that comes with a wedding?"

"What would you know about it? You've never proposed to a woman in your life—and proposing a one-night stand doesn't count."

I scratch my neck and my cheek, because I've suddenly developed itches all over my body. "You make me sound like a right bastard. If you think I'm such a dick, why haven't you flown over here to drag me away from Elena's best friend?"

"Relax, Reese, it was a joke. You're not a dick." He hesitates before asking, "Do you like Arden? Really like her?"

"What, are we children now? Do I like her. What an asinine thing to ask." I have no idea why the question makes me uneasy, or why I get snarky with Chance because he asked it. I also have no bloody clue why I say, "Do you think Elena would mind if I wanted to, um, date Arden?"

Since we're already in a relationship, why do I need to ask permission? If Elena vetoes the idea, I won't stop dating Arden.

But I want to know what my brother thinks of it.

Yes, I'm an idiot.

"Date? You?" Chance laughs, but it doesn't sound like sarcasm. "Never thought I'd see the day. I'll ask Elena."

I hear a noise like he's holding the phone away from his face, then he shouts his fiancée's name.

"Chance, I didn't mean you should actually ask her—"

But it's too late. He's not listening to me anymore, and I hear Elena's lovely laughter when he asks her, "Would you mind if Reese dates Arden?"

"Of course not," she says. "As long as he behaves."

"I'm afraid that's not at all likely."

"That's not funny," I say so loudly I'm almost shouting. "You two are off my Christmas list. And forget birthday presents too."

Elena laughs again, and Chance joins her this time.

The bloody pair of them. I'm seriously concerned about whether Elena and Chance mind if I date Arden, and they're laughing at me.

"It's okay," Elena says. "But Arden's the one you need to ask for permission."

Maybe I should admit to them I've already done that, she's already said yes, and we're already dating and in a relationship. No, that would be too much honesty.

Some sort of movement catches my attention out the corner of my eye, and I glance toward the hallway.

Arden has come out of her room wearing nothing but those damn plaid knickers and a bra so thin I can almost see through it.

"Got to go," I tell Chance and Elena. "See you in New Hampshire."

I hang up and jump off the sofa. "Good morning, Arden."

"Morning." She yawns, holding a hand over her mouth. "What were you yelling about?"

"Nothing. I was on the phone with Chance and Elena."

"You should've let me say hi too."

"Sorry. They were in a sarcastic mood, anyway."

Arden strolls over to the sofa but sits on the coffee table instead. She yawns again. "How's the happy couple?"

"Irritating and nosy."

She tilts forward to touch my knee. "Did you tell them anything about us?"

"If you mean did I tell them we slept together and it was the best sex ever, no." Now I'm squirming, because her hand on my knee has suddenly become the biggest turn-on in history. Her lack of substantial clothing doesn't help either. "But if you mean did I tell them we're dating, the answer is yes. I asked if Elena would mind that."

"What did she say?"

"That I need to ask your permission, not hers."

Arden smiles in *that* way, the one that dimples her cheeks and makes me want to drag her into my arms for a kiss so deep it'll be almost like sex. "You already have my permission, Reese, for dating and a relationship. Date me like crazy, date me like you really mean it, like you—"

"I understand." And I'm positive whatever she'd wanted to say next would've diverted all the blood in my body to one particular region. "Let's go out for breakfast this morning."

"Ooooh, I'd love that."

"You should pick the restaurant, love. I don't know what's good around here."

She rubs her palms together, her tongue poking out between her teeth while she considers the options.

And I want to fuck her. On the coffee table.

Instead, I tell her, "Why don't you think about where you'd like to eat while you get dressed?"

"Okay." She hops off the table and heads for the hallway, but she stops halfway there to glance back at me. "I really like you, Reese. You're lots of fun and so sweet. Not at all what I thought a player would be like."

She goes into her bedroom and shuts the door.

Arden likes me.

Chance had teased me about whether I like her, and I'd gotten snarky about it. How do I feel about Arden Clover Pesti?

I like her too. A lot.

For some reason, I feel the need to change into nicer clothes, so I hurry down the hall. My old jeans and T-shirt don't seem good enough for a formal breakfast with Arden. Unless she plans to take me to a fast-food restaurant. Then I'll be overdressed.

I freeze halfway down the hall. What am I going to wear?

Oh no. I've turned into a woman.

The door to Arden's bedroom flies open.

She's standing there wearing denim cut-offs that barely cover her arse and—what do they call those things?—a tube top with the tiniest sweater I've ever seen. It covers her shoulders, though barely, and stops a few inches past her underarms. The thing looks like it shrank in the wash, or maybe it's a doll's clothing.

But it's her feet that make me choke on my own tongue.

She wears heels so slender I can't imagine how she stays upright, and so high that I think she might be taller than I am while she's wearing those shoes. They have thin straps to hold them on her feet, and to show off her lavender-painted toenails. Those high heels are the sexiest thing I've ever seen.

And I want to lay her down on the floor, toss her legs over my shoulders, and take her right here. I want that even more than I did a few minutes ago. So badly that I'm fisting my hands and gritting my teeth.

"Ready to go?" she asks. When she looks down at my feet, she says, "You might want shoes."

"I know." The words come out as a growl. "I was going to change into something… else."

"Don't bother." She scans me up and down, her lips curving into a sensual smile. "You look plenty hot already. I can feel my panties melting as we speak."

I cough into my fist, mumble something even I can't understand, and rush into my room to get my shoes. When I return to Arden, she's leaning back against the wall beside her bedroom door, swinging a tiny lavender purse in one hand.

Somehow, I prevent myself from mauling her and offer her my arm like a gentleman would, though my feelings toward her at this moment are the exact opposite of gentlemanly.

Chance and Elena are fine with me dating Arden, so maybe they won't mind if I…

No, no, no, and absolutely fucking no, you flaming arsehole.

I ignore my carnal urges and escort Arden to the cafe she's chosen for us. It's a casual place, so I fit right in. Arden couldn't fit in if she tried, and I don't want her to. It's not because she's "kooky," as she calls it. She's a stunning woman, and whenever she smiles, the entire world lights up. Her laughter should be patented as a cure for depression. It makes me feel good every single time.

While I listen to Arden ordering our breakfast, I can't help smiling. She's thoroughly adorable. And yes, I let her order for me, because I'm that sort of modern man. You know, the type who lets women do everything for him, not because he's lazy but because he knows that's what women like. I respect female power and all that bollocks. I'm an evolved man.

All right, the real reason I let her order for me is because I love the sound of her voice.

But I do respect her, which feels strange. I like her, I respect her, and I want to shag her. Maybe I have evolved.

We eat crepes filled with sliced bananas and served with caramel sauce on top. I'm not sure about this meal, but I give it a go—and end up liking it. Arden makes me want to try new things. I gave her a new experience too, but I'm not sure sex is as important as trying new foods or going to new places I never would have visited on my own. Like the science museum. Or Coney Island.

The thought stops me. I'm holding a forkful of banana-filled crepe to my lips but can't move another millimeter to eat it. Going to a museum is better than sex? Did I just think that?

"Are you okay?" Arden asks. "You look kind of pale all of a sudden."

I shake off my disturbing thought and look at her. She's so bloody beautiful. And sweet. And clever. She's the most perfect woman I've ever met.

"Reese?"

"Sorry, fine, yes." I shove the forkful of crepe into my mouth and chew it while I try to figure out what's happening to me. Once I've swallowed my mouthful of food, I attempt to speak without sounding like an idiot. "There's nothing wrong with me. I had a strange thought, that's all."

"What were you thinking about?"

You. But I don't say that. I can't. My vocal cords refuse to produce any sound. I shrug and eat the rest of my breakfast, consuming bite after bite without any space between bites so I can't be tempted to blurt out stupid things.

Arden watches me for a moment, seeming a bit suspicious, but soon she goes back to eating her crepe. She doesn't ask me about my strange thought anymore.

I let her take me wherever she wants to go. We visit every tiny, off-the-map tourist spot in the city, and some in New Jersey too, and I love every second of it. Arden can turn anything into a wildly entertaining experience. I even agree to pose for a selfie with her, like we did at the science museum, because she seems to love those. I slip an arm around her waist and smile while she takes the picture.

And I haven't even thought about shagging her in at least two hours.

Chapter Fourteen

Arden

When we get home, after a day of sightseeing and eating and laughing and kissing, I text Elena the selfie of me and Reese that I took today. She responds a few minutes later with a series of emojis that all include hearts or kissing lips. I'm not kissing Reese in the photo, so I have no idea why she's doing that.

I reply with an emoji of a face with its tongue sticking out.

Yeah, maybe we're both reverting to junior high behavior.

But it's not funny at all when Elena calls me a few minutes later and says, "You're sleeping with Reese, aren't you?"

"What?" I can play dumb, even though I'm not.

"Come on, Arden. You took a selfie with him, and I've never seen you do that with any of those other guys."

"Reese is fun. I really like him. Is that a crime?"

"No, but hearing you say that only convinces me even more that you're sleeping with him."

"As if that's any of your business." Though she can't see it, I sit up straighter in my puffy armchair and lift my chin. "For your information, I am not currently having sex with Reese Dixon."

"Not currently?" Elena's tone changes, becoming softer and throatier, the way she always talks when she's discovered a juicy secret. "Does that mean you've done it already? Or you're about to do it?"

I sit there with my mouth open while I try to figure out how to avoid answering without Elena realizing that's what I'm doing. I suck at subterfuge, though. Always have.

My silence speaks all the words I didn't want to say.

"Okay," Elena says, "it's none of my business. But at least tell me one thing. Was it good?"

"If the question of whether I'm sleeping with Reese is none of your business, how is it okay to butt your snoopy little nose into the question of whether he's good in bed?"

"You're right. I'm sorry." She sighs with phony disappointment. "I guess I'll have to infer the answer. Chance is such an incredible lover that I'm betting Reese is fantastic too."

"Elena, honestly." I relax into my chair, twirling a lock of hair around my finger while I remember exactly how fantastic Reese was on the night we slept together. "I'm betting Reese is way better than Chance."

"Let's agree to disagree on that one."

We chat a little more, then say goodbye.

I hear the shower running in the bathroom, and my mind decides now is the right time to give me a high-definition, 3D, surround sound mental movie of Reese in the shower. Naked. Wet. The water drizzling down his body. Steam billowing around him while he runs his hands all over himself, spreading soapiness on all those muscles…

Lucky suds.

The doorbell chimes, and I drag my butt out of the chair to shuffle over to the door. I'd rather sneak into the bathroom and join Reese in the shower. But I behave like a good girl and open the door to greet whoever's there.

"Arden, darling," my grandmother says, opening her arms in an invitation to hug her.

I give in and accept the embrace. "Hey Grams, what are you doing here?"

She keeps her hands on my upper arms, though we're an arm's length apart now. "You look tired."

"Gee, thanks. You look old."

Her laughter is big and uninhibited, like always. She knows I'm joking because my lips turn up at the corners, and besides, she knows me too well to think I'd insult her. Ever since I hit puberty, Grams and I have enjoyed ribbing each other, affectionately.

Celeste Arnaud keeps her blonde hair cut short, but since she has lots of curls, it doesn't look severe. And yeah, she dyes her hair. Though she's in her seventies, she has zero wrinkles—thanks to a fantastic plastic surgeon. Her designer dress cost more than my first car. Grams stays slim too, and her perfect figure makes me look chunky.

I'm not jealous. I like my body, and I love Grams to pieces.

She cocks one hip and sets her hand on it. "Well, may I come in? I'm not used to hanging around in dank hallways."

I wave for her to enter and shut the door behind her. "It's not dank. This building is perfectly nice."

"Nice?" She stops between the bar and the sofa, swiveling her gaze this way and that. "I don't understand why you won't stay at my townhouse. This apartment is a hovel."

Yeah, I love her despite the fact she's an enormous snob.

"This is Elena's old place," I tell her, "and I like it here. It's cozy."

Grams closes her eyes and shakes her head. "Dear lord, how did I end up with a heathen for a granddaughter?"

"Watch it, Grams. I'll tell you all about the greys again."

She smiles and puts an arm around my shoulders. "All right. If you're happy, I'm happy."

"Thank you."

"But honestly, I don't see the appeal." She waves her other arm toward the windows in a grand gesture. "You don't even have a proper view."

The bathroom door opens, and Reese moseys into the living room. He stops at the other end of the sofa from us, and his gaze switches back and forth between me and Grams.

He's wearing nothing but a towel, slung so low on his hips that it seems like it'll fall off if he coughs.

Grams notices him—how could she not—and her brows lift. She rakes her gaze over him from head to toe, taking special notice of his towel and the bulge that's hiding underneath it. When she gets to his face, her lips kick up at one corner.

She looks at me. "Well, I believe I'm starting to see the appeal of this apartment."

Reese is looking at me like he wants to know what's going on.

"Um," I say, fumbling to get my brain in gear and stepping away from my grandmother. I point toward the half-naked elephant in the room and say, "Grams, this is Reese Dixon. Remember Chance, Elena's fiancé? Well, he's Reese's brother. Reese, this is my grandmother, Celeste Arnaud."

He strides across the room to shake my grandmother's hand. "It's a pleasure to meet you, Ms. Arnaud. Arden has told me all about you."

"Call me Celeste." She holds on to his hand even when he tries to pull it away. "Arden has told me nothing at all about you, but I think I can guess why. Gorgeous and British. I bet my granddaughter isn't a virgin anymore."

"Grams!" I almost shout it, and the syllable ends on a squeak.

She waves a hand like she's dismissing my freak-out. "It's about time you crossed that bridge, darling. But I'm dying to know more about your new… friend."

Grams slides her gaze up and down his body again, and I swear to God she licks her lips.

I'm helpless to squelch my indignant tone. "Grams, for heaven's sake. A senior citizen shouldn't be ogling a hot young man. What would Granddad think?"

"Your grandfather knows I only want him. Why should he care if I window shop?"

Reese is grinning.

And my cheeks are on fire.

"I have a fabulous idea," Grams says. "Let's all go out to dinner at my favorite restaurant. I have a standing reservation with a table on hold for me anytime."

"Your favorite place is super swanky," I say, "and I don't have fancy clothes. I doubt Reese does either."

"We'll stop off at Armani on our way to the restaurant." She ogles Reese again. "I'm sure he'll look scrumptious in a designer suit."

Once Grams makes up her mind, there's no stopping her. I let her take us out for shopping and dinner. Reese puts on jeans and a T-shirt for the trip to Armani, but nobody in the ultra-chic store cares about what he's wearing. All the female employees vie for the chance to get Reese fitted for a suit.

Maybe I get a teensy bit jealous of those pretty, stylish babes fawning over him. Maybe. Just a smidge.

And damn, he really does look scrumptious in an Armani suit.

Over dinner, Grams and Reese talk. A lot. I sit there like a lump in a designer dress, not saying a word. Normally, I have no problem with jumping right into a conversation, but tonight I've become a mute. Grams can't resist teasing me and Reese with sarcastic and often suggestive comments throughout dinner. This is her way of being friendly with my new boyfriend. She keeps telling him how amazing I am too, which is kind of embarrassing.

When Grams drops me and Reese off at the apartment, she whispers in my ear, "I approve."

"Um... thank you?" I honestly have no clue what I'm supposed to say to that, and dumb words are all I can come up with.

"He's gorgeous, yes," she continues, "but he's also whip-smart. Just like you. It's a perfect pairing, like chardonnay and escargot."

"I hate escargot. Slimy little dead snails in my mouth? Ew."

"Fine, forget the snails. I'm trying to say you and Reese are perfect for each other."

She kisses my cheek, says "adieu" to Reese, and leaves.

I'm alone with Reese. Sure, I've sort of lived with him for a week and a half, but tonight being alone with him feels different. He charmed the socks off Grams, or rather, charmed the silk stockings off her. She has never liked any guy I've ever dated, but she fell for Reese at first sight.

Kind of like I did.

He stands there across the sofa from me, in his Armani suit, looking so outrageously yummy. I want to eat him up, but something has changed between us. Something I can't yet identify. I know how to hunt down facts, no matter how obscure, but understanding this thing between me and Reese has me stumped.

Because I've never felt anything like it.

We're dating. We're in a relationship. But I don't know where this is all leading.

He sweeps his gaze over me while he unbuttons his jacket. "You are so beautiful, Arden."

"It's the dress. Armani makes any girl look fabulous."

"You've got it the wrong way round. *You* make the *dress* look fabulous."

"Thanks." My cheeks warm, but not with embarrassment. The heat of his gaze penetrates me, sizzling on my skin and deeper into the most intimate places. "You make that suit look so damn hot."

He crooks a finger, beckoning me to come to him.

I cross the distance between us, my gaze never leaving his, and stop right in front of him. Inches separate us, and I swear I can feel the heat of his body radiating into me.

Reese settles his hands on my arms, gliding them up and down so slowly and with such decadent tenderness that his touch sets off a tingling sensation in its wake.

"Mm," I hum, laying my hands on his chest. "I want you. Tonight. Please, Reese, don't say no again."

He kisses my forehead, my nose, my lips.

I slide my hands inside his jacket and push it off his shoulders. He takes his hands off me only long enough to shed the jacket. I grasp the knot in his tie and work on freeing it, while he showers light little kisses on my temple, down my cheek to my jaw, and on the sensitive spot just under my chin. The thought of being with him again, of feeling and touching his body again, excites me so much that I moan even while I undo his tie and toss it away.

When I grasp the top button on his shirt, he lays his hand over mine to stop me.

"Maybe we shouldn't," he says. "I want you so much it's killing me, but Chance and Elena—"

"Will get over it. They're cool with us dating, so they'll be fine with us getting it on once they realize it's none of their damn business."

"You're probably right." He slides his hands up to my shoulders and down my back to the top of the zipper on my dress. "Can't care anymore. I need you, all of you, naked, underneath me, on top of me, everywhere."

"Oh yes." I unhook the buttons on his shirt one by one, my fingers grazing his skin as I go, loving the way his breath catches. "Let's stop thinking and just do it."

He drags the zipper down, inch by inch, nibbling my earlobe while I shiver from the feel of cool air on my back and from knowing I'm about to have what I've craved for days. Him. Inside me.

I push the shirt off his shoulders.

Reese shrugs out of it, then plucks the straps of my dress off my shoulders. The dress drops to the floor, leaving me in only my flimsy lace panties and bra. I've worn the semitransparent one he liked this morning, or I assume he liked it. When he saw me in it, his eyes had glazed over, and his mouth had fallen open.

He takes in the sight of me, running a hand over his mouth.

Then he sweeps me into his arms and rushes me into the bedroom.

Chapter Fifteen

Reese

I sprint into Arden's bedroom and lay her down on the bed. The covers are over it, but I'm so excited about making love to her that I don't care. I pull her knickers off, then reach under her body to undo her bra and get rid of it too. She lies there naked, with the sweetest smile on her face, and bites her lip in the way that always makes me want her.

All right, I want her every second of every day. She doesn't need to bite her lip to get me worked up. But watching her release that lip little by little makes me even harder for her.

The thought I had a minute ago comes back to me. I want to make love to her, that's what I'd thought. Make love. Have I ever used that phrase to describe sex before? Maybe once before, and I think it was earlier today. Arden has done more than drive me to break my promise to Chance, or to break my habit of never staying in a woman's bed all night. Because of her, I want more than sex. Only with her.

A strange sensation hits me, like a hard thump to the chest. No one has struck me, though. This feeling is inside me. When I look into Arden's eyes, the thump turns into pressure, but it doesn't feel bad. I like the sensation.

"What's wrong?" she asks.

"Nothing. I'm fine."

I kiss her, softly at first, savoring the taste of her lips and the slickness of them. She tastes like strawberries, but I know from kissing her *a lot* that she likes to use flavored lip balm. Yesterday, it was peach. I take her bottom lip between my teeth and lick it, then slip my tongue between her lips in quick, light strokes until she moans and grasps my head, mashing her mouth to mine.

When I pull my head away, she makes the sweetest frustrated noise.

"Only a minute," I say, standing up, "and then I'll give you what you deserve."

She trails her fingers over her body, from her breasts all the way down to the hairs that mark the part of her I know will be slick and hot and ready for me. Arden gets aroused faster than any woman I've ever known, and I love that about her. I love her body. I love her smile too, and her laugh, her energy, her enthusiasm for everything, and—

I stop in the middle of taking my trousers off and stare at her. The things I've been thinking…

"You look anxious again," she says. "Like you did a few minutes ago. What's wrong, Reese?"

"Nothing."

"Bullshit." She pushes up on her elbows. "Tell me. Please. Have I done something wrong? Something that makes you not want me anymore?"

Christ, she thinks I don't want her? She'd have to be blind not to see exactly how much I crave her, because my cock is stiff and bobbing, all but waving at her to come and get it.

I finish undressing and crawl up the bed to straddle her body, gazing down at the face of the most beautiful woman in the world, the one who thinks I don't want her anymore. I sweep hair away from her eyes and kiss the tip of her nose. "I will always want you, Arden. Always. But I've been having these thoughts that I'm not used to having, and it's… confusing."

"What kind of thoughts?"

How do I explain this without sounding like a moron?

Maybe it doesn't matter if I sound stupid. Maybe she needs to know, even if the thought of telling her makes me slightly nauseous and more anxious than I've ever been. Don't I owe her that much? She gave me her virginity.

I take a deep breath and tell her the truth, though I have no idea what's about to come out of my mouth until it happens. "I love you, Arden."

Her face goes blank. She doesn't blink.

Why did I say that? We've known each other for less than two weeks. She must think I'm insane.

"I know it's awfully soon," I say, "but I—well, I feel—it, uh, well..."

Her lips curve upward millimeter by millimeter, easing into a smile that broadens into a grin so bright it lights me up too. "Relax, baby. I love you too. So you can stop stammering, even though seeing you flustered is completely adorable."

Only five of the words she spoke reach my brain—"baby" and "I love you too." She called me baby. And she *loves* me.

"Are you sure it's not too soon to say that?" I ask.

"No, baby, it's not too soon. I believe in love at first sight, so a week is actually kind of slow."

I kiss her and gaze into her eyes like a lovesick fool. And I don't even care. I'm a fool, and it feels good. I keep kissing her while I glide a hand down her body, slipping it between her thighs to caress her, stroking her folds and rubbing her clit with my thumb. Her back arches, and her mouth is torn from mine. I draw her earlobe into my mouth, still rubbing and stroking her, loving the way her breaths shorten and she grips my shoulders.

Her mouth falls open. She closes her eyes, lost to the pleasure that's building inside her.

"Arden," I murmur, then I claim her mouth in a deep kiss, thrusting my tongue in time with the movements of my fingers.

When she whimpers into my mouth, I know she's on the edge.

I am too, ready to explode and I'm not even inside her.

Her entire body goes rigid.

"Let go," I say. "Come for me, Arden. Don't hold back. I want to see and hear and feel all of it."

The climax seizes her hard and fast, and her knees bend toward her body like strings inside her legs have been cinched up tight. She squeezes her eyes shut, her nails digging into my shoulders, and she cries out.

I keep stroking her until she's done, mesmerized by the way her expression changes from shock to blissful pain to sheer pleasure, and finally, the most exquisite look of satisfaction. Her hair is a mess, her cheeks are pink, and she's still breathing hard. But I've never seen anything so perfect in my life.

She reaches down to close her hand around my cock. "I want my mouth on you."

"Have you ever done that before?" Since she was a virgin until I showed up, I doubt she's ever done what she's suggesting. Not that I don't want that. I do, of course. I'm a man, and we always love a good blow job. "You don't have to do that to make me happy. All I need is you."

"But I'd like to give you the same kind of thing you give me. I want to try." She lets go of my cock, her shoulders hunching. "But you're right, I've never done it before."

"Let's hold off on that until another time. I want to teach you all about sex. But for tonight, let me take the lead."

"Okay. You're in charge, baby."

My pulse speeds up, like it does every time she calls me that. "I love the way you keep calling me baby."

"You've called me 'love' several times."

"Have I? Maybe I fell for you at first sight after all."

She slides a hand into my hair and pulls me closer. We kiss more, kiss like we mean it, like nothing else matters except this night, in this room. The rest of the world might as well have evaporated, because all that exists for me right now is Arden.

I lay my body on top of hers.

She whispers against my lips, "Condom."

"Fuck."

I jump off the bed, find my trousers, and dig a condom out of the pocket. When I try to open the packet, I fumble it. The condom flies out of my fingers and lands on Arden's belly.

Laughing, she sits up and shimmies across the bed to sit on the edge. "Let me help. I've practiced putting condoms on a zucchini."

"A zucchini?"

"Mm-hm." She rips open the packet and begins rolling the condom onto me. "I knew eventually all that practice would come in handy."

The feel of her delicate fingers on my dick is making me breathe harder. She's got a look of intense concentration on her face, but it gradually gives way to a hunger that makes my balls tighten. By the time she gets the condom on, I've lost my breath completely. She's stolen it, and I don't mind at all.

Arden crawls across the bed on her hands and knees, giving me a perfect view of her arse—and her tits that hang down and sway with every movement of her body. She pulls the covers off the bed and lies down on her back.

"I'm ready," she says, almost purring those words. "Are you?"

"Ready, randy, and raring to go." I make my way up the bed to her, hovering over that luscious body, drinking in the sight of Arden for a moment before I lower myself onto her. "Am I too heavy?"

"No, I like it. Make love to me, Reese. Please."

She opens her thighs for me.

Braced on my elbows, I ease inside her. She feels so damn good, the way her body fits me like a glove. I take my time, letting us both experience every sensation, watching her face while I push in and pull out. The scent of her desire fills the air and intoxicates me, so much that I want to go faster, go harder, make her bounce and scream. But I need this to last. I need to feel her around me for as long as possible so I can memorize every second of it. This time feels different, more meaningful, and I never want it to end.

She wraps her legs around me, wraps her arms around me, and gasps every time I push inside her sweet, willing body.

"Arden," I whisper.

"Oh Reese, baby, I love you."

Those words rush through me like the most addictive drug on earth. I accelerate the pace, taking her harder, pulling out further before I plunge into her again. She clutches me tighter, not only with her legs and arms, but with her inner muscles too. God, she's close. I could push her over the edge so easily, but I want this to go on and on.

I rest my forehead on hers and force myself to slow down.

Her eyes are half closed and glossy. Her breaths tickle my skin every time she gasps. And that's all she does now. Gasp. Moan. Gasp again. My name spills from her lips a few times, and the wet sound of our joining echoes through the room.

Arden peaks in slow motion, her body clinching me tighter and tighter while her mouth falls open and her eyes flutter shut. When the full force of her release takes hold, she cries out and holds on to me with her entire body. I lift my head enough to see her face, so I can witness the intensity of her pleasure.

"Reese," she says, and it's a strangled cry.

I can't hold back any longer. I straighten my arms to get more leverage and thrust into her. Once is all it takes. I let go and lose myself inside her, pouring out everything I have while I shout her name.

Then I fall on top of her. Not the most romantic ending, but I seem to have lost all control over my muscles.

Arden combs her fingers through my hair, sighing with contentment. "You're the best lover in the world."

I chuckle. "You've never been with anyone else. How do you know I'm the best?"

"Because I do." She molds her lips to mine, but only for a moment. "I don't need to screw every man on earth to know that nobody else can compare to you."

"All right, have it your way." I slide off her body to lie on my back beside her, then link my hands under my head and smirk. "I'm the best ever."

"Don't get cocky about it."

"Why not? I'm always cocky, and you love it." I glance at her, still smirking. "Your grandmother thinks I'm amazing too."

Arden rolls onto her stomach, propped up on her elbows. "I love everything about you, Reese. You're more than amazing in bed. You're amazing, period. That's why I love you, because you're so sweet and kind and smart and funny."

"I love you for the sex."

She elbows me in the side. "You're supposed to tell me all the things you love about me, not go all sarcastic Brit on me."

"Maybe I should keep fucking you until you give up and admit that being British is what you love most about me." I palm her arse. "My accent is the reason you've never been able to keep your hands off me."

"Never denied that." She tips her head down and looks up at me through her lashes. "Keep talking. Your accent drives me wild."

I pull her on top of me. “Why don’t I recite dirty limericks?”

“Yes, please.”

I do that, and more.

Chapter Sixteen

Arden

The day after the night when Reese and I said the L word to each other, we fly to New Hampshire. On my grandmother's jet. She's coming to the wedding too, and no self-respecting billionaire travels commercial. Grams has the jet decked out with shades of pink and sunny yellow, including the seats. Reese doesn't seem to care about the girlie interior. He plops right down on the pink sofa, gesturing for me to join him.

I do. Duh. He's gorgeous, sexy, and British. Of course I do whatever he wants me to do and love every second of it. Unfortunately, all we can do on the plane is sit there and talk. Grams and Reese trade racy jokes, and I laugh. I don't know any dirty jokes or limericks or anything like that, so I let them have their fun.

Chance and Elena pick us up at the airport in a limo. We'll be staying at a bed-and-breakfast, since Chance and Elena's house isn't big enough to accommodate everyone. The rooms they do have are spoken for—by Elena's brother and his girlfriend, and by Dane Dixon.

"Why did Dane get first choice?" Reese asks, pretending to be offended.

At least, I think he's pretending.

"He's older than you," Chance says, "and he's much less irritating. Besides, I don't need to listen to you and Arden getting stuffed every night."

I raise my hand like a kid in school. "What does eating too much have to do with anything?"

Chance bursts out laughing. So does Reese.

Elena smacks her fiancé's arm. "It's not Arden's fault Reese never told her getting stuffed means having sex. You Brits have a responsibility to educate Americans in your bizarre language."

Okay, at least I now understand what Chance meant. And yes, Reese and I agreed to act like mature adults and tell Chance and Elena we're sleeping together. We broke the news as soon as we saw them. They've been much cooler about it than I expected, but I guess they finally realized Reese and I are old enough to make our own decisions.

The limo has two bench seats, so Reese and I sit on one side while Chance, Elena, and Grams sit on the other. Granddad went to Stockbridge to collect my parents, and the three of them are already here in New Hampshire.

"Whatever you want to call it," Chance says, "I don't want to hear my brother and his girlfriend doing it."

"Jealous, are you?" Reese says. "I've been declared to be the best lover on earth, so you're right to feel inferior."

"Who declared you're the best? That sounds like a rigged contest."

I raise my hand again. "Me. I told him that."

Elena rolls her gaze toward the roof and shakes her head, though it's sarcasm rather than annoyance. "Oh please, like you're an expert."

"Tell you what," I say, leaning forward to give her my best look of mock seriousness, "I'll let you have sex with Reese so you can find out for yourself."

Reese grins.

Chance throws an arm around Elena and pulls her against him. "My fiancée is not having sex with anyone else. But I'll get a leg over with Arden to prove her wrong about my brother."

Reese scowls, and I don't think it's sarcasm. "No, you will not."

"Not grinning anymore, are you?" Chance says to his brother—with a smug smile on his face. "Calm down, Reese. I don't want to steal your girlfriend. Elena's all I need."

Chance kisses Elena's cheek.

Reese hugs me to him for the rest of the car ride.

We get to relax for about an hour, lying in bed watching true crime shows because, apparently, that's the only channel our TV will let us watch. After that, I go with Elena to the dress shop where she bought her wedding gown so she can have the final fitting. She wants my advice about the veil—to wear one or not to wear one, how long should it be, et cetera—and I offer my opinions. Honestly, I think she wanted me here only because she's nervous. She adores Chance, but getting married is a big deal.

And she misses her mom. I know she does. Elena's mom passed away years ago, but not having her around for the wedding is hard. Maybe a best friend isn't a substitute for a mother, but I do my best to make this special for my best friend and to fill in for what Elena's lost. Her dad left when she was little, so her only family is Kyle. My dad will give Elena away during the ceremony because my parents love her like she's their daughter.

While I'm with Elena, Reese is with his brothers. Chance doesn't want a bachelor party, and Elena doesn't want a bachelorette party, so the groom is hanging out with his brothers and Kyle Linwood. They have a good time, based on how much those guys are smiling when Elena and I meet up with them.

That night, Reese and I have our own kind of fun. He teaches me more about sex, and every lesson ends with me shouting his name. He hasn't taught me what I really want to know. In fact, he seems embarrassed every time I ask him about oral sex. He's not at all shy about that when he's giving it to me, but he doesn't want to talk about how I could do the same for him. Guys are so weird.

The next day, we head to the wedding rehearsal. Dane is Chance's best man, and I get the feeling Reese is a little hurt by that. Reese will stand at the altar with his brothers, but he wasn't chosen to be best man. I'm Elena's maid of honor, but she doesn't have any other bridesmaids, so nobody's jealous of me.

Later, we all head to a restaurant for the rehearsal dinner.

I manage to get a few seconds alone with Chance and Elena, so I tell them I think Reese feels spurned. Maybe I shouldn't tell them that, but I can't imagine Chance wants his little brother to feel left out. It turns out I'm right about that, and Chance has a private conversation with Reese that makes him much happier. I don't know what Chance said, but I'm starting to see why Elena loves him. He's one of the nicest people I've ever met. He loves his family, especially his brothers.

Chance might be on my top ten list of nicest people, but Reese is *the* nicest. He'll always be number one on my roster.

When we get back to the bed-and-breakfast, we're both so exhausted we strip off our clothes, crawl under the covers, and pass out.

In the morning, I get to share a steamy shower with Reese. And I don't mean only that the water is hot enough to make real steam. We generate plenty of that on our own.

Today is the wedding. My best friend, the woman who's like a sister to me, is marrying the love of her life. And I'm in love with her brother-in-law. Or rather, the guy who will become her brother-in-law later today. It all seems kind of like a strange dream, but one that's also so wonderfully perfect.

I watch from the altar in the quaint little church while Elena walks up the aisle. Everyone in attendance is watching her because she's the most beautiful bride anyone could imagine. Her dress is lacy and swishy and makes her look like a princess—not that I've ever met a princess. I glance over at Chance and see him wiping at his eyes like he might cry at the sight of his bride coming toward him, about to vow to love, honor, and cherish him. He'll promise the same thing to Elena, and I know he'll mean it.

Reese is wiping at his eyes too.

Though I never would've pegged him as the sentimental type, I like knowing that he can get emotional when it's appropriate. It makes me love him even more.

And yeah, I'm crying. It's no discreet tearing up, either. Uh-uh, I'm full-on crying with tears running down my cheeks by the time Elena reaches the altar.

My gaze swerves to Reese right when he looks at me. He smiles and mouths, "You are beautiful." He's so full of it, because my eyes must be red and puffy, but I know he honestly thinks I'm beautiful, no matter what.

We keep looking at each other throughout the ceremony. I hear the wedding spiel, but I don't really pay attention to it. I keep thinking about the past couple weeks and how my life has changed so much. I'm in love with a British guy. He lives in England. I live in America. Will he ask me to move over there to be with him? What will I say if he does? Do I want to leave my home country? It wouldn't be fair to demand he leave his country to be with me. I have no idea how we'll work this out, and honestly, it's too soon to be worrying about that. But I can't stop the thoughts, the worries, that ricochet through my mind.

I glance at Chance and Elena right as he puts the ring on her finger. He's already wearing his wedding band, so they kiss. It's the sweetest, most romantic thing I've ever seen. And I cry. Again.

Then it's over.

Reese and I ride in the limo with Chance, Elena, and Dane. My parents and Grams are in another car, so I don't see them until an hour later, what with all the guests at the reception and the food and the dancing and—Jeez, weddings are such a production. I dance with both Chance and Dane, as well as my dad and their dad and a few guys I've never seen before. Apparently, they're friends of the Dixon brothers. I don't get to dance with Reese until another half hour later, when he tracks me down at the buffet table, claims my hand, and leads me out onto the floor.

It's magical, dancing with Reese. He keeps one hand on the small of my back, his other hand holding mine in the usual dancing posture. We spin around and around, floating across the floor inside our own little bubble, in time with the romantic music provided by a string quartet. He looks so dashing in his tux, like a prince or a duke or whatever they call those royal people over there in England.

But the song ends, and Elena waves at me. It's more like flapping her hand wildly. She wants me to go over there.

"The bride is summoning you," Reese says.

"Yeah, I haven't gotten to talk to her since we left the limo."

"Well, go on." He gives me a gentle push. "Don't leave the bride waiting."

I kiss him and hustle over to Elena. "What's up?"

"We haven't had time to talk about anything except the wedding since you got here. I wanted to catch up with you before Chance and I leave on our honeymoon."

"You know I haven't been up to much. Decompressing after Ecuador, mostly."

She gives me a funny look, like she's not sure if I'm full of shit. "What about you and Reese? How serious is it?"

I'd guessed she would ask this question sometime, but I didn't think she'd do it tonight. I have to answer honestly, even if she thinks I've gone insane. "I love him, Elena."

"Chance said Reese told him the same thing. He's completely in love with you and will do whatever it takes to make your relationship work."

Whatever it takes? Reese said those words? My heart does a strange pitter-patter thing when I hear that.

Then I remember something I've been meaning to ask her but haven't had a chance until now. I sidle up to her, hooking my arm under hers, and ask away. "Can I get your advice on a sex issue?"

Elena laughs, though it's almost a whisper-laugh. "You know, I've been waiting for the day you'd ask me that, but now that you have, I feel a little weird about it."

"If you'd rather not—"

"Ask me, Arden."

"Have you ever given a guy a blow job?"

She's just taken a sip of her champagne and splutters, like a cartoon character. "What? Well, yeah, I have."

My best friend is flustered by my question, but I charge ahead anyway. Desperate times or whatever. If Reese won't share the deets with me, I have to get them from Elena.

"Does Chance like it when you do that for him?" I ask.

Her smile is knowing, and she glances at her hubby who's across the room from us. "Oh yes, he likes it."

"Good. Can you give me some pointers?"

Her attention veers back to me, and her brows crinkle. "Pointers? We can talk about that another time, okay?"

"Can't wait. I need to know how to give Reese a blow job tonight."

"What's the rush? From what I hear, you two have plenty of fun already."

Yeah, my parents and Grams have made sly comments about the noise coming from the room Reese and I are sharing. They're happy for us, but they can't resist teasing us about it.

"Please," I say to Elena, "I need your help. A few pointers, that's all I'm asking for."

"Okay." Elena leans in and whispers in a conspiratorial tone, "Here's how you make a man's eyes roll back in his head…"

Chapter Seventeen

Reese

I'm talking to Celeste Arnaud and her husband when her granddaughter waltzes up to me and says, "Come with me, please. Grams, you don't mind, do you? I need to have a private moment with my honey."

Her honey? It sounds silly, but I like it. "Baby" is still my favorite thing Arden calls me, but I like any word she wants to apply to me.

"Go on," Celeste says. "I've been wanting to chat with Dane, anyway. Oh, there he is at the buffet table. I'll go grab him before someone else does."

All the women who aren't here with a significant other want to dance with my brother. I don't get it. He wears glasses, doesn't like to talk about himself or his work, and doesn't have the stellar sense of humor I have. Then again, I'm taken. So the ladies here have to settle for Dane.

I'm joking. You know that, right? Well, mostly joking.

My sexy little American leads me away to… a coat closet. No joke. She drags me in there, shuts the door, and pushes me back against the wall.

"What are you about?" I ask. "If Dane told you I was flirting with other women, he's a bloody liar."

"Oh, I know you'd never do that." She kneels in front of me. "I'm not going to yell at you. I have something else in mind."

"What are you—" My voice dies when she unzips my trousers. "Arden?"

"You wouldn't tell me how to do this, so I had to ask Elena." She pulls my dick out of my trousers and takes it in both her hands. "I want to do this for you, Reese."

"Uh, not here. Let's wait until we get back to the bed-and-breakfast."

"No more waiting." She licks the head of my blossoming erection. "You're coming for me whether you like it or not."

My laugh comes out choked and a bit panicked. "Arden, you don't have to—"

She kisses my cock and pumps it with one hand. "Why do you keep saying no? I thought guys *loved* getting blow jobs."

"Normally, yes, but not at my brother's wedding." My head falls back against the wall, and I groan when she takes me in her mouth. "Arden, please. Let's do this later."

Does that stop her? Of course not. She's determined, and when Arden wants something, I have no willpower to make me say no. This is even hotter than when she prances around in her virtually invisible underwear. Her mouth, her silky tongue on my skin, it's more than any normal human male could possibly resist. Not that I'm normal. Not that she's an average girl. And the way she slides her tongue over me while she sucks and pumps with her hand…

I grasp the back of her head and stop trying to resist.

The door flies open. Someone gasps. Another someone yelps.

Arden jerks away from me, falling backward and landing flat on her arse.

I stare at the man and woman who have stumbled onto our liaison in the coat closet, but I can't speak. Arden made sure of that.

The two people look familiar. My brain is thoroughly muddled by what Arden just did to me, so it takes me a moment of gawping to realize who these people are.

Arden's parents.

"Mom, Dad," she says, scrambling to her feet. "Why are you in the coat room? Are you leaving already?"

"No, flower girl," Arden's mother says. "We saw you and Reese come in here, and it seemed like you were taking a long time. We thought we should check on you, just in case."

"In case of what?" Arden says with a smirk. "In case we got trapped in coat cocoons spun by invisible aliens?"

Mr. Pesti glances at me—not my face, but down much lower where I'm still swinging free. He coughs and swerves his attention away. "Sorry we interrupted. Let's get back out on the dance floor, hey Tally?"

Arden's mother nods to her husband. "Oh yes, I'd love another dance with that hunky Dane."

For bizarre reasons I'm certain even she doesn't understand, Arden announces, "Reese is way hunkier than Dane and a better dancer."

"I'm sure he is," Tally Pesti says, winking at me.

Arden's parents leave the coat room.

She kneels in front of me again, stubbornly determined to finish what she started. The interruption from her parents has left me much limper than before they threw the door open.

I cup Arden's face in one hand. "Let's get back to this later, when we're alone in our room. I want to teach you more of my favorite things."

"And then you'll tell me how you like to be given a blow job?"

She looks so earnestly concerned about understanding what I like that I can't help dropping to my knees and kissing her, with only my lips. Anything deeper and I'll give in to her request right here in the coat room.

I rest my forehead against hers. "Yes, I'll tell you everything you want to know. Later."

Her smile, so bright and excited, makes my heart swell.

When I lead her back out into the reception hall, I glance around and spot Arden's parents dancing, smiling and laughing while they glide across the floor. Next, I see Chance and Elena dancing. She has her head on his shoulder, and he leans his head against hers while his eyes drift shut. His smile is the picture of contentment, and I wonder if I ever look that way when I'm with Arden.

I notice Dane and Celeste having a lively conversation at the periphery of the dance floor. They're not dancing, so I get curious about what they're discussing and decide to drag Arden over there. Is Celeste flirting shamelessly with my brother? I know her flirtations are only that, nothing more. Her husband is doing something that vaguely resembles the moonwalk with the girlfriend of one of Chance's mates. Celeste keeps glancing at her husband, her smile broadening every time she sees his strange dance moves.

Arden's family is full of nutters, I decide, but they're the friendliest, most lovable bunch of nutters I've ever met. They're clever too, a fact that most people probably overlook. Celeste is a billionaire, after all, and her husband serves as her chief operating officer.

We reach Celeste and Dane in the middle of their conversation.

"It's intriguing," Dane says, "but I'm used to running the business all on my own."

"And I don't want to change that. Think of me as your mentor and silent partner."

"What are you guys talking about?" Arden asks, her gaze flitting between her grandmother and my brother.

Celeste touches Arden's arm. "I'm propositioning Dane."

My brother opens his mouth two seconds before he manages to speak. "She means a business proposition. I've been telling Celeste about my company."

"Grams," Arden says, "you own a cosmetics company. Dane makes vibrators."

My brother clears his throat. "Sexual wellness devices."

Celeste makes a dismissive hand gesture aimed at Arden. "I know all about that. What do you think we've been chatting about? I've already expanded into perfume and jewelry. This is the next step in the evolution of Bonsoir. Our corporate motto is 'be your best after dark,' which ties in nicely with what Dane's company does."

Arden still seems confused. I'm right there with her. Cosmetics and vibrators? I have a sudden vision of women putting on makeup, spritzing on perfume, and grabbing their sex toys. Yes, it's important to look and smell your best when you're having a wank.

"You seem dubious," Celeste says to me. "Don't you want your brother to succeed? I can make him an instant billionaire."

I laugh, assuming she's not serious.

No one else is laughing.

"Wasn't that a joke?" I say. "Nobody becomes a billionaire overnight."

"Dane will," Celeste says. "With my help and the power of the Bonsoir brand behind him."

Christ, she means it. My brother, an instant billionaire? I can't decide whether to be happy for him or terrified of what Celeste will do to launch his company into the stratosphere.

She moves behind me and Arden to come up alongside me, clapping a hand on my shoulder. "I have a proposition for you too, Reese darling. How would you like to be my new vice president of advertising? My president of advertising will be retiring in a year or two, and I need to groom his replacement."

"Vice president? I've been a copywriter. And I'm twenty-four."

"So what? You're whip-smart, and I trust you. Trust is the scarcest commodity in business." She leans in to whisper in my ear. "If you're worried your coworkers will be jealous, let me handle that. I'm a genius at calming down internal strife."

That statement might've sounded arrogant coming from anyone else, but Celeste makes it sound reasonable. I believe she must be a genius at that, exactly as she claims.

"She really does rock the employee relations," Arden tells me. "Grams is great with people."

Celeste pats my shoulder. "Who knows? By the time you and Arden have your first baby, you might be the president of advertising at one of the world's largest corporations."

"Baby?" I splutter. "We're dating, Celeste. Only dating."

And I'm head-over-heels in love with Arden, but that doesn't change the fact we're still dating. It's been two weeks since we first met.

My girlfriend reaches across my body to smack her grandmother's arm. "Stop that, Grams. You're scaring Reese."

"I'm not scared," I announce.

Celeste kisses my cheek. "I'm looking forward to having you as a grandson-in-law."

"Grams!" Arden chastises.

"Still not scared," I declare, rather enjoying being sandwiched between beautiful women.

Dane, who's smirking, pushes up his glasses. "Arden, maybe you'd like to test drive some of my latest devices before they hit the market. I'm sure you'd have insightful feedback."

Arden tries to speak, but I jump in before she can get one word out. "No, she does not want to test your ruddy devices, Dane."

"What's wrong, Reese? Afraid she'll like my toys better than yours?"

I know he's having me on and trying his best to annoy me. Normally I wouldn't care. But whenever one of my brothers makes a slyly suggestive joke about my girl, I get… irritable.

This time, Arden beats me to the punch. "Oh, trust me, Dane. There's zero chance of your devices outdoing Reese. No offense. I'm sure your doohickeys are fantastic, but nothing compares to a real man."

I puff up like a turkey spreading his feathers for his mate. Yes, I'm a ridiculous arse. I don't care, because Arden announced to my smug brother that I'm a real man.

Dane chuckles. "Glad to hear it, Arden. Reese deserves a woman like you."

"What kind of woman am I?" she asks, and she's serious about the question.

Only Arden could try to give me a blow job in the coat room, then turn around and innocently ask my brother what sort of woman he thinks she is.

"The best sort," Dane says. "I've never seen my brother this happy before. You and Reese are perfect for each other."

Chance and Elena approach us then and announce they're leaving to start their honeymoon night. Tomorrow, they'll fly to the south of France for the first leg of their international holiday.

Arden and I go back to the bed-and-breakfast and get on with our lessons.

She is perfect for me. I think I've known that since the first time I saw her.

But it takes me three more weeks to summon the nerve to ask her the inevitable question. We're in my old bedroom in my parents' house, since the cottage we bought a few miles away isn't ready for us to move into yet. We're planning to alternate between America and England, so we can see both our families as often as possible. Arden has always worked from home, and Celeste loved the idea of her new vice president of advertising trading off stints in the New York and London offices.

Chance, Elena, and Dane are here for the weekend too. The newlyweds are just back from their honeymoon, and strangely, I want to hear all about it.

But right now, I'm sitting on the edge of the bed with Arden kneeling between my legs. She licks her lips and hums with pleasure.

"Mm, Reese," she says, "you always taste so damn good."

That's right. She now loves to get my cock in her mouth, and I love the way she does it. I'm a man, of course I love a blow job—especially from a stunning, passionate woman whom I just happen to worship.

I rub my thumb over her lips and kiss her forehead. "I love you, Arden. You really are the right woman for me."

"And you're the right man for me." She sits back on her heels and skims her hands along my thighs. "I love you too, baby."

"Will you marry me?"

Bollocks. I'd planned this whole speech, even practiced it in front of a mirror, but the words burst out of my mouth like my tongue has a mind of its own.

Her eyes bulge.

"Sorry," I say, covering my face with my hands. "That's the worst proposal ever, isn't it? I swear I had a romantic version ready to go, but—Gah, it flew out of my head."

Her soft, gentle hands peel mine away from my face. She smiles with such sweetness and tenderness that I get a strangely pleasant ache in my chest, the sort only she can give me. "I don't care how you propose, Reese. It's what you have in your heart that matters. And yes, I absolutely, positively want to marry you."

"Really?"

"Yes, really," she tells me with a laugh while she takes my face in her hands. "You're so cute when you're flustered. It makes me want to get it on with you."

"That would be my choice for how to celebrate our engagement."

She scuttles backward on her knees and flaps her fingers, telling me to move back.

I scramble backward up the bed until I bump into the pillows.

Arden hops up and takes a running leap at the bed. She lands straddling my calves, then crawls up my body until her face hovers above mine. "Ready to get hot and sweaty?"

"For you, always."

We decide to announce our engagement over dinner and even get Arden's parents and grandparents, along with Elena's brother, to join in via video call on three phones. Elena and Arden both shriek and jump up and down. Chance and I exchange amused looks, like we can't believe our women are so barmy. Who are we kidding? We love their enthusiasm.

Dane watches it all with one brow raised, acting like he thinks we're all barking mad.

I walk over to his chair and whisper in his ear, "Watch out, Dane, you'll be next."

He snorts. "Like hell I will."

"Famous last words, mate. Famous last words."

Love the

Hot Brits

series?

Visit

AnnaDurand.com

to subscribe to her newsletter

for updates on forthcoming books in this series

&

to receive a free gift for signing up!

Anna Durand is a bestselling, multi-award-winning author of contemporary and paranormal romance. Her books have earned bestseller status on every major retailer and wonderful reviews from readers around the world. But that's the boring spiel. Here are the really cool things you want to know about Anna!

Born on Lachland Air Force Base in Texas, Anna grew up moving here, there, and everywhere thanks to her dad's job as an instructor pilot. She's lived in Texas (twice), Mississippi, California (twice), Michigan (twice), and Alaska—and now Ohio.

As for her writing, Anna has always made up stories in her head, but she didn't write them down until her teen years. Those first awful books went into the trash can a few years later, though she learned a lot from those stories. Eventually, she would pen her first romance novel, the paranormal romance Willpower, and she's never looked back since.

Want even more details about Anna? Get access to her extended bio when you subscribe to her newsletter and download the free bonus ebook, *Hot Scots Confidential.* You'll also get hot deleted scenes, character interviews, fun facts, and more!

Visit AnnaDurand.com to sign up.

www.ingramcontent.com/pod-product-compliance
Lightning Source LLC
Chambersburg PA
CBHW070445170726
48291CB00005B/1604

* 9 7 8 1 9 4 9 4 0 6 3 0 6 *